CW00692813

# BLINDFOLD FROM THE STARS

*By the same author*

THESE SAVAGE FUTURIANS

THE TIME MERCENARIES

DOUBLE ILLUSION

TWIN PLANETS

*Philip E. High*

# BLINDFOLD FROM THE STARS

LONDON : DENNIS DOBSON

All persons and events portrayed in this book are fictitious. Any resemblance to persons living or dead, or actual events, is purely coincidental.

*First published in Great Britain 1979 by*
*Dobson Books Ltd, 80 Kensington Church Street, London, W8*

*Printed in Great Britain by*
*Bristol Typesetting Co, Ltd,*
*Barton Manor, St Philips, Bristol*

ISBN 0234 72142 1

# CHAPTER ONE

*The conquest of a galaxy is relatively easy providing the aggressor has the necessary technology and more important, a safe method of overcoming possible opposition without bleeding to death in the process.*

*The Race of Asdrake—pressed by a population explosion—had found one, as simple as it was ruthless.*

*When a planet suitable for occupation was discovered, it was first checked and, if containing intelligent life, checked still further.*

*A number of lone natives were kidnapped, studied and finally dissected.*

*Then the second part of the plan went into operation. A large number of faster-than-light missiles were released from the home system. These missiles broke up on penetrating the atmosphere. They contained mutated micro-organisms which directly attacked the human brain. The victims became lethargic, slowly incapable of movement and finally died. The period from infection to death was about thirty days.*

*This slow process more or less ensured the preservation of vital installations and the careful shut-down of power sources.*

*The Asdrake, however, waited until the bodies were decomposed and the smell of death long departed—say two years.*

*The Asdrake liked the method. They could fight if they had to but were inherently lazy. Besides, why louse up a habitable world with a lot of craters and razed cities?*

*They had recently selected their latest victim but here complications had arisen.*

*The Supreme Commander looked at the message from the Department of Biological Warfare and exhaled noisily through broad flat nostrils.*

*Side-effects! What side-effects? The method had worked successfully on twenty-two occasions, why should it fail now?*

*He flicked on the information switch with a furry finger.*

*PLANET 5/6/9. SECTOR 88. SUN SYSTEM 46. 'TSEUDEC' (NATIVE NAME: 'EARTH').*

*CULTURAL LEVEL: 6*

*TECHNICAL LEVEL: 33*

*The Supreme Commander switched off and studied the cautiously worded message again. It suggested that further biological research was necessary before assault. The Department was not happy, the native brain deviated in some respects from the norm. It was possible, therefore, that routine methods would be less successful than heretofore.*

*The Supreme Commander snorted the equivalent of 'So what!'*

*A large proportion of the population were bound to be affected and, if they were not, he could take a class 6/33 culture apart with one ship.*

*As for side-effects, he was convinced—correctly—that the*

*Department of Biological Warfare only assumed possible side-effects.*

*He crumpled the message in his hand and threw it over his shoulder.*

*'Attack will proceed as scheduled by orders of the Supreme Commander—.'*

*Casualties from the epidemic were astronomical yet, in complete paradox, failed to kill a single human being—the side-effects took care of that.*

As with all major catastrophes, there were survivors and Bill Travers—William J. Travers, Sales Representative—was one of them. He worked for a vast international chemical combine, now defunct, but he had yet to find that out.

Travers was thirty-three, dark haired and not unhandsome. He worked hard enough at his job to hold it down but no more. He was, he was aware, singularly unambitious, at least, in respect of work. There was so much in life, so many worthwhile things to experience which the rat-race prevented. Other men could struggle to become area managers or executives—picking up their ulcers en route—but that was not for him, to hell with it.

Life, civilization and an unhappy marriage ending in divorce had made him cynical but, at the same time, philosophically shrewd.

Was the rat-race really a race for visible goals or were the contenders, although unaware of it, running away from something?

To Travers it was a moot point and many of his views were equally disturbing.

When the infection began, he was staying at a small inn

several miles from the nearest city. There were several reasons for this. One, he didn't like cities. Two, it was cheap and, three, he was doing all right with the proprietor's daughter. He also liked the inn's position. It was cosseted between low green hills and overlooked a small pleasant lake.

He awoke that particular morning with the feeling that something was wrong. It was an obscure sort of feeling and he was unable to put his finger on it. He went quickly through the previous day. Yes, all orders had been confirmed and dispatched by post, not that.

He rolled over and glanced at his watch. Eight-thirty! He should have been in his car and on the road half an hour ago. Where was his morning coffee? Why were the curtains still drawn?

He rose, drew back the curtains and stared out of the window.

Outside it was raining dismally, the lake was puckered with rain drops and shrouded in mist.

He shrugged. To hell with it. He washed, dressed, shaved unhurriedly and went downstairs.

The inn was empty.

He walked round the building several times, shouting: 'Marion!—Bob, Mr. Wallace!'

No one answered and he returned inside, puzzled.

He raided the refrigerator, helped himself to some cold chicken and made himself a coffee.

The feeling of unease had increased but he assured himself it was due to the emptiness of the inn. Probably a perfectly natural explanation, family crisis or illness involving a close relative, such things happened.

He finished his coffee and drummed his fingers absently on the edge of the table, conscious of a growing depression.

What a day, what weather and what a bloody future. Out on the road, year in and year out—for what? One never had the opportunity or the cash to visit strange places or swim in tropical waters.

He let his mind wander. Silver sand, sunlight, a lagoon—he loved swimming—a coral island. It was nice to dream and it wasn't too much to ask, was it? God, he wished he was there now—.

There was no sensation of transition or of time. One fraction of a second he was sitting at the table and, in the next fraction, he was standing in bright sunlight.

Silver sand sloped downwards to blue still waters and a sand crab scuttled by, pincers warningly erect. Far out, the rollers hurled themselves in white spray against the reef.

He stood still but his eyes moved. To his left and to his right, the shoreline curved towards the reef. Palm trees swayed in a slight warm breeze, sea birds circled far out over the lagoon.

Travers was one of those people who remain calm in moments of crisis but get the shakes hours later. His brain was working coolly but a little numbly.

He didn't tell himself that it couldn't be because it *was*. He could feel the heat of the sun through his jacket, he could feel it on his face.

He bent down, picked up a handful of sand and let it trickle through his fingers. Then he walked down to the sea and put his fingers in the water. It was warm, almost tepid but he had forgotten his desire for a swim.

He forced himself to reason. He had wished he was here and he was here. Things like that didn't happen but this time it had.

Could he wish himself back?

He wished.

He was sitting at the table in the inn.

Had it been a dream?

No, there was silver sand on the carpet near his shoes and his jacket was still warm.

The implications hit him suddenly. Supposing he had wished—*no!*—or—*no!*

He was afflicted with terror—suppose—suppose—dear God.

He rose, helped himself to a whisky from the bar and poured a generous measure down his throat.

It seemed to steady him a little but his terror remained.

He sat still for a long time trying to regain a measure of calm. It was, he decided eventually, something best forgotten. There was, no doubt, some explanation but he didn't want to dwell on it. Better put the whole incident behind him. A fantastic incident had occurred, probably under unusual circumstances of which he was unaware.

There was nothing he could do about it and no one would ever believe him. The best thing to do was to forget it, push it out his mind as much as possible. He didn't want a repetition. That sort of thing was enjoyable in fairy tales but it frightened the guts out of you in real life.

Got to get back on the road, back to all the grind—it

had certain attractions now. After a few calls and a few rebuffs, he would soon revert to normal.

He walked out to the car park at the rear of the inn, more conscious than ever of the dullness of the sky.

High on the roof, a solitary seagull squawked depressingly and monotonously.

The sound added to Travers' sense of despair and desolation. Every damn thing was adding its quota to the intolerable pressure building up inside him.

Abruptly he lost his temper.

'Ah, drop dead, damn you!' he said savagely and aloud.

The bird stiffened, then fell slowly sideways. He watched it roll untidily down the roof in a series of small bounces. It landed with a faint thud at his feet, eyes glazed and claws in the air.

He stared at it for a long time. He was trying to relate and, at the same time, trying not to relate his words with the actual happening.

After some minutes, he went inside again and poured himself another whisky. The bottle neck rattled against the glass and a lot of whisky ended up on the floor.

Travers was cold inside yet his face felt as if it had been splashed with water. Sweat crawled down under his collar causing an irritation of which he was only half aware.

If only there was someone to talk to—Marion? No, she was all right in bed but—face it—she was stupid. Bob? No, not him either, he would simply stand there with a silly grin. Mr. Wallace, the manager, yes, fat and jovial but no bloody fool.

The trouble was, Mr Wallace was nowhere around. He

was a man who would *listen*, dear God, he wished he was here now—.

There was a sudden and heavy impact beside him. Four bottles, some glasses and a tray of sandwiches fell to the floor.

Travers turned, startled. Then he put his hand over his mouth in a desperate attempt to stop himself vomiting.

Wallace was back—what was left of him.

Travers recognized the gold ring on the third finger of the left hand. He recognized the digital watch and the blue suit.

There was not much else left to recognize. What remained of Wallace was draped over the bar like a torn and bloody sack. His right arm was missing and something had torn off his head.

Travers picked up a full bottle of whisky and walked stiffly from the building. He felt numb and his surroundings seemed unreal.

He put the bottle carefully in the back of the car—might need the lot later—and started the engine.

It occurred to him only briefly that he was well above the legal alcohol limit for driving but he no longer cared.

He drove down the short drive to the road and turned left for the nearest city.

Before he had covered a hundred yards, he was compelled to mount the grass verge for a vehicle blocking the road. One door hung open but the car was empty.

Two minutes driving brought four more and then there was a pile-up involving six vehicles. Five of the wrecks were empty but the sixth held a dead man. He had gone through the screen and lay sprawled on the bonnet.

Travers got past by driving into a ploughed field. Once past, he put his toe down and raced for the brow of the hill where the road joined the main highway.

When he got there, he stamped on the brakes, knuckles white on the steering wheel.

The main highway looked like a bombed transport division.

Vehicles lay slewed at all angles and, close to him, a big blue car had tried to climb a telegraph pole.

Some distance away was a gigantic pile-up involving at least forty vehicles. Two huge trucks had apparently collided head-on and following traffic had ploughed into the wreckage.

In the distance, pillars of black smoke crawled slowly upwards in the still air. In many places cars were burning and he could see several still bodies in the various wrecks.

Travers realized abruptly that whatever had happened had not been a wholly personal thing. Some major tragedy had overtaken the human race, at least in this part of Canada.

Some time during the night, something had struck. It had passed over the inn while he slept, taking with it Mr Wallace, Marion and poor, simple-minded unshaven Bob.

It had passed over this highway, over major and minor roads, leaving death and destruction behind it.

He shivered and glanced uneasily upwards at the grey drizzling sky. Was it still hanging around in case it had missed something—himself, for example?

He looked at the highway again and, in the distance, something caught his eye. He thought at first that it was a redness from one of the fires but it wasn't.

This thing was drifting above the wrecked vehicles as if searching. It was round and scarlet like a hot coal but contained within a circle of black. A sullen roundel with a black rim or, he thought morbidly, a bloody eye in a black socket.

Suddenly and without warning, his nerve snapped. He slammed the car into reverse and collided with an abandoned vehicle. Barely aware of it, he shot forward in a wild U turn, knocking down a signpost in the process.

He had no idea where he was going, his only thought was to get away.

The speedometer was quivering on ninety and the hedges were a blur before his panic evaporated. He slowed down just in time to negotiate the pile-up in which the dead man was sprawled.

He decided to drive on past the inn, back the way he had come yesterday—with variations. Some of the journey had included the main highway.

Fortunately he knew the country roads and tracks intimately. A man like himself, with inclinations for the clandestine, had to know his way around, he thought, sourly. Maybe that knowledge would now save his life—maybe.

God, what was that thing he had seen? He had no doubt it was completely alien. Although it had been almost a mile away, he figured it was about fifteen feet in diameter. Large enough to carry, say, three men—men?

A thought occurred to him. How could a sphere have a black rim? If it had a visible rim, it must be a disc, like, for example, one of his wheels. He was oddly unconvinced, it had *looked* like a sphere.

He realized he was dwelling on the subject because the implications frightened him.

He had read stories about interstellar invaders and dismissed those stories as fantasy. However well written and however plausible, it just couldn't happen.

He frowned. This was familiar reasoning. Violence happened to other people, road accidents to other drivers and riots occurred in other countries never one's own. This was a protective philosophy and not a rational one.

He turned down a side road which was almost a track, confident that the chance of meeting or seeing another vehicle was virtually nil. He had driven along this road at peak holiday periods without passing a living soul.

The road climbed steadily through thickly wooded country and there was a comforting arch of branches above him.

He came to an open glade and turned into it. A few minutes walk through the trees would bring him to an area where the ground sloped steeply away to the flat lands below. In this weather the glimmer of the distant ocean would not be visible but he should be able to see the city.

He climbed out of the car, conscious that his legs felt rubbery and weak.

As he walked, he watched everything intently, not only from fear of attack but for assurance. The trees were real, weren't they? He touched them gingerly. Rooks still cawed as they flew above. A wood pigeon perched on a branch eyed him briefly then continued to preen its feathers. The wood smelled the same, dead leaves and small twigs crackled beneath his feet.

One hot day he had brought Marion out here, ostensibly for a picnic. It seemed centuries ago now.

He came to the edge of the slope and stood staring in front of him. The city and parts of the highway were visible, great columns of black smoke rose from the city and formed a pall above it. It looked as if about a quarter of it was on fire.

He could see no sign of the disc thing by the highway, maybe it had gone elsewhere.

Travers tried to put out of his mind a mental picture of silent alien vessels stabbing their shining lances at the cities and highways below them.

Funny he had heard nothing during the night, he was not a heavy sleeper and yet—. He shrugged. No doubt, if he lived long enough, everything would be explained.

He turned away, deciding to take the alternate path back to the car. It led through a huge clearing where a budding forest fire had been stopped by local volunteers some two summers past.

He walked quickly, suddenly aware that he was hungry. A chicken leg and a couple of slices of ham was hardly a solid meal, was it?

He remembered he had something in the car. A slab of chocolate, sandwiches and a flask of coffee. The sandwiches would be stale, the coffee cold but, put together, it would fill a gap.

As he approached the clearing, he came to an abrupt stop. Bacon! Someone was frying bacon. No doubt it was another refugee like himself who had had the time to bring some supplies with him.

Yes, wood smoke! Maybe there were eggs too! At that

moment, all else seemed subjugated to a solid familiar breakfast.

He hurried towards the clearing and tripped over a fallen branch. He fell heavily, barking his knee on an exposed tree root.

The pain saved his life because he stopped and looked ahead.

The clearing was swathed in a tangle of threads. Threads which shimmered and danced, even on this dull day, with the iridescent beauty of a thousand rainbows.

Travers didn't ask himself what the threads represented, it was, all too clearly, a web.

He didn't wait to see the spider. A creature which could fill a five hundred foot clearing with such a mesh would obviously regard a human being as a quick snack.

Travers ran back the way he had come and hurled himself into the car, slamming the door behind him.

He gunned the motor and lurched out of the glade, soil spraying from spinning tyres.

The next time he stopped, it would be in an open space where he could *see* what was around him. The trees fell away a couple of miles on, he'd stop and eat there.

As he drove, points about the incident began to fall into place. The spider which had built that web was an intellectual cut above a normal spider. There had been no frying, no wood smoke and no smell of bacon.

The spider, if spider it was, had perceived the predominant thought in his mind and somehow contrived a bait. Had he, Travers, been thinking of a naked woman, no doubt, the most luscious blonde he could possibly conceive would have been standing seductively in the middle of the glade. This spider not only built a web but supplied the correct bait in the form of an hallucination.

Travers was not aware of it but he was beginning to acquire survival faculties fast. He had a photographic memory and the rare ability to profit from experience.

He was still unaware of the change although his thoughts were fully concerned with survival and rapid adaptation to conditions.

He was, by nature, a realist and he knew that many of the things he had hitherto taken for granted, no longer applied. As far as he was concerned, heroes had ceased to exist. If survival dictated that he run like a scalded cat, he was going to do exactly that. One stood and fought only when there was no alternative.

There were no restraints. He was not bound to go forward into danger as, for example, a soldier who was compelled by duty to press on regardless. Nor was there anyone to cheer him, not that it would make any difference. There was only one primary concern and that was staying alive. He was honest enough to admit these things to himself without justification, years of conditioning were falling away rapidly.

He noticed that the trees were beginning to thin and he slowed the car accordingly. Here he would see what was on either side and, at the same time, if anything was hanging around in the sky.

Once on the low plateau, he pulled the car under the branches of a large tree where it would be invisible from the air. Then he looked about him carefully for signs of danger.

He knew the area. Grass, moss-covered boulders and widely spaced immense trees. The ground was undulating, bisected with rock shoulders and fretted with cleft and hollow.

Difficult tank country, he thought, irrelevantly but a God-send for defending infantry.

Some six miles distant, he saw, the level land dropped almost sheer for six hundred feet.

Still in the car and still watching carefully, he ate the stale sandwiches, washed them down with cold coffee and chewed some chocolate. Better save some, food was going to be a big problem in the near future.

Finished, he climbed cautiously out of the car and looked about him.

After a brief search, he found a piece of fallen branch which would serve as a staff and was heavy enough to break a skull. He didn't want to use it that way but he would if he had to.

The solid weight of the branch gave him a certain comfort. It was probably useless against some of the things around but, with it, he felt less vulnerable.

Now for a brief look around. He picked a tree in the distance, knowing that from there, he could see the track curling downwards for several miles.

He glanced upwards at the still drizzling sky and hoped it would not become a downpour. One hour of heavy rain and the dirt road would become impassable.

He reached the tree about ten minutes later and climbed the slight rise on which it was standing.

He reached the top and stopped dead.

Below, a bare hundred feet away on flat open ground,

three cars were drawn up neatly side by side as if the owners had decided to stop here and picnic.

No one appeared to be near them but their very presence struck Travers as slightly improbable. Who the hell would park three large cars out here in the middle of nowhere? Particularly so in the middle of an interstellar invasion or whatever it was that was going on.

Had they been a small group of army vehicles or even the overloaded cars of fleeing refugees, the picture would have made sense. These cars, however, were outwardly immaculate and looked as if they had been driven here straight from the showroom.

Taking advantage of every possible cover, he edged closer.

The first car was a superb Rolls Royce with a British registration. The second was Cadillac's newest and plushest model about which he had been reading a bare week before.

The third, in silver-grey, was the newest and most luxurious model ever built by Mercedes.

Travers stared at them, trying to relate their perfection, sleekness and spotless condition with the present crisis.

'Magnificent are they not?' said a man's voice behind him.

# CHAPTER TWO

Travers spun round, his staff half raised.

'Where the hell did you come from?'

'Did I startle you? Please accept my apologies.'

Travers lowered his staff only slightly. The man facing him was tall, greying and distinguished of feature. There was, however, something about his eyes, something staring and glassy, which made Travers feel a certain reserve.

The man's suit was obviously Savile Row but the long black cloak with its high collar and scarlet lining was out of keeping with it.

'I was up in the mountains,' explained the man. He made a vague gesture to barely visible snow-capped peaks in the distance.

'You will appreciate that I am here incognito but you may call me Alcott—Roger Alcott.'

'My name is William Travers.'

'Of course, of course, now that you remind me. A being in my position has so many, many subjects you understand.'

Travers nodded, aware that his smile of agreement had a certain stiffness. The man was an obvious nut.

'You were admiring the cars?'

'Er—ah—yes.' Now what?

'I have a Cadillac,' said Alcott. 'But I always wanted a Rolls and a Mercedes, now I have them.'

He made an indolent gesture of deprecation. 'The world is mine to command,' he explained.

He glanced at his watch. 'Two thirty, time for lunch. You, Travers, as my loyal subject, will eat with me. However, before doing so, I have a small experiment to undertake—this way.'

He led the way to a large rock and stopped by it.

'If you will be good enough to place four of those large round stones on that rock—yes—those, thank you.'

He smiled briefly. 'I have just flung myself from the highest mountain—you will recall the story, no doubt—the angels of heaven supported me lest I dash my foot against a stone. This, too, is part of the temptation.'

He assumed a commanding pose with folded arms.

'Become bread!' he said in a resounding voice.

It took some time for the truth to penetrate Travers' mind. He blinked several times, to make sure it was not a trick of the light.

*Where the stones had been were four loaves of bread.*

He went a little closer with the uneasy feeling that he had been hypnotically tricked.

They *were* loaves but, to Travers, somehow the apparent miracle had gone disturbingly awry.

The first loaf was brown, the second looked stale, the third obviously so with betraying spots of green mould. The fourth, however, was the most bizarre of all.

It was a wrapped loaf and bore the label 'A COUNTRY-KISSED LOAF FROM UNITED BAKERIES.'

Travers began to edge backwards slowly and, he hoped, unnoticeably. The sooner he got away from this nut the better. The apparent miracle, too, had him worried because, somewhere, something was almost clear yet still eluded him.

'Only a demonstration of my power,' explained Alcott, apparently untroubled by the incongruity of a wrapped loaf. 'As you have observed, it can be done.'

He smiled in an oddly sly way. 'You have, no doubt, penetrated my incognito by now.'

Travers, who had been debating whether to clout Alcott over the head or run for his life, suddenly found a solution. You humoured lunatics, didn't you?

He fell to one knee and bowed his head.

'Sire,' he said.

'Ah, well done thou good and faithful servant.' Alcott was beaming. Then, conversationally: 'Only the chosen are permitted to look upon the face of God, you know—you may rise.'

Travers obliged with a furtive look round for the nearest cover. He might still have to use the staff and make a run for it.

God, however, in the shape of Roger Alcott, seemed unaware of the black thoughts in his subject's mind.

'I command the winds and the tides and all the peoples of the Earth.' He raised his arms. 'Storm!'

The sky darkened almost immediately, the wind howled, spots of rain fell about them.

'Storm begone! Clear sky and sunshine!'

Slowly the clouds cleared, watery sunshine broke through which gradually increased.

'Now we will eat,' said Alcott.

Travers' quick wit came to the rescue.

'Sire, I am honoured but I must return. I have thy work to do.'

Alcott beamed. 'But of course, my son, my blessing be upon you.'

Travers crossed himself—he hoped, correctly—and walked backwards for what he hoped was a respectful distance. Then he turned and walked rapidly away.

Once out of sight, however, he ran as if all the devils in hell were after him.

He kept running until he reached the car, then leaned on it panting. God, he was out of condition, irrelevant thought, really. Too many things to think out, like how to stay alive. Wonder if tip-top health would give me an edge?

Once he had regained his breath, he climbed into the car and tried to relax. Just how much, in the way of shocks, could the human nervous system take?

He fumbled in his pockets for a cigarette then crushed the empty carton in his hand. He hadn't smoked the whole damn lot since this morning, had he? He had no recollection of doing so but, perhaps under stress—.

Blast! Not even the consolation of a smoke but under the circumstances he needed more than one packet, didn't he? The way things were going, he needed twenty and a couple of bottles of whisky for good measure. He wished—.

There was a thud on the passenger seat beside him and he felt his muscles lock in sheer terror. What now?

Without moving his body, he managed to look sideways and suddenly went limp.

Scattered untidily on the seat beside him were twenty packets of his favourite brand and two full bottles of Scotch.

Uneasily he touched the bottles, they were real. So were the cigarettes. Shakily he unwrapped the cellophane and extracted a cigarette.

Getting the cigarette into the flame of his lighter posed a problem. His hand was agued and, in the end, he was compelled to hold his wrist with his left hand.

At last! He inhaled deeply and scowled at the whisky. Not that yet, got to think. Got to make himself calm and *think.*

Go back. He'd wished himself on a coral island and found himself on one. He'd wished for cigarettes and whisky and they'd materialized beside him.

Again, supposing he had wished for—*no*!

Got to watch that, never mind what caused it for the moment. Got to think out some sort of safety system, something to stop the odd wish which might plunge him into—*no*!

He fumbled in the glove compartment for his order book and turned to a blank page.

He wanted a word, a key word, preferably an unusual word. A foreign word for preference—languages had always fascinated him—how about the German 'to open'? Yes—

He began to scribble, shakily.

Some ten minutes later, he was still scowling at the result but decided it would have to do.

He read: 'Unless my command, or wish, is prefixed by the word *Aufmachen*, it is to be ignored.' Then he read it aloud and with force.

He inhaled deeply several times before he said: 'I wish I had another packet of cigarettes.'

Nothing happened.

'*Aufmachen*! I wish I had another packet of cigarettes.'

There was a thud on the seat beside him and another packet appeared.

Travers relaxed a little. Rule one had been learned and a safety-catch had been contrived.

He could now let his mind wander without fear of self-destruction.

Supposing he wished himself dead, on another world or that familiar cliché, that the earth would open and swallow him up?

Got to keep thinking. If only he wasn't so bloody shaky and—let's face it—scared out of his wits. Did this thing work psychologically?

He stared unseeingly in front of him, debating the possibility of induced peace but too nervous, as yet, to risk an experiment.

Suppose, whatever it was, didn't work on those lines? Suppose the attempt turned him into a posturing lunatic like Alcott?

Finally he picked up his order book and began to outline another command. This had to be just right, it had to have balance. It had to strike a compromise between bland and dangerous calm and exigences of what had become a virtually alien world. A world he no longer understood and whose laws had changed beyond rational adjustment.

After much scribbling, scratching out and re-writing he arrived at what he hoped was the answer he wanted.

*I wish to be mentally and physically calm enough to reason clearly about the problem which faces me but not to the detriment of natural caution and alertness.*

It was a clumsy sort of command, he decided, but he knew exactly what it meant and that seemed to be important.

He read the command aloud, prefixed by the command word.

The effect was not immediately apparent but a few seconds later he felt his physical tension begin to drain away and his thinking processes become clearer.

He lit another cigarette with a hand that was wholly steady and leaned back in the driving seat. He was glad to note that he was still alive to possible danger but without the same crushing fear.

The process of thinking was far easier now and a lot of facts began to relate to one another.

In the first place, something had happened during the night, probably some sort of alien attack. That disc thing over the highway seemed proof enough of that. On top of that, they'd done something—perhaps used some sort of weapon—which had changed the natural laws which had always applied to Earth.

Overnight, man had acquired, or had forced on him, new supernormal faculties. It was, perhaps, ironic that these same faculties were the ones some had claimed to possess, others had studied and a large section of humanity indirectly worshipped for countless centuries.

He, himself, had acquired—was telekinesis the right word? He was sure it meant moving objects from one place to another without known physical cause. He also had teleportation which was moving himself—had he anything else?

Travers decided abruptly that he didn't want to know, not yet anyway. He had too damn much on his plate already without nosing around for more.

For some—like Alcott—the sudden acquisition of such faculties had been too much. He had not only gone insane but believed he could turn stones into bread.

The factor which had eluded Travers at the time suddenly fell into place. *The bread had come from somewhere.*

If proprietors of stores still existed, one of them was four loaves short.

No doubt the three cars had been 'acquired' by the same means, hence their spotless condition.

Travers thought, with a slight feeling of guilt, that someone else was minus twenty-one packets of cigarettes and two bottles of whisky.

Thoughts seemed to be tumbling into his mind now. If he could tell a seagull to drop dead, someone could wish the same thing on him.

He spent five minutes drawing up a defensive command. The first man who tried that trick on him was going to be sadly disappointed. God, the thought of such powers bestowed on the utterly ruthless was terrifying.

Another disturbing thought occurred to him—*to whom, or what, did he give the command*?

It could, of course, be his subconscious mind but he'd like to be *sure.*

The trouble, as he saw it, was that the damn thing was on a sort of hair-trigger. It was a dicey sort of thing in any case and something he must treat with considerable reserve.

A tinge of unease touched him suddenly, followed by a deep sense of guilt.

All he'd thought about was himself, keeping *himself* alive but there were *others*.

Perhaps the saving facet of Travers' nature was his faculty for self-criticism. He was, he knew, lazy, self-indulgent and a womanizer.

On the other hand, he was intense about some things. He loved children and animals and was apt to take a swing at anyone who attempted to hurt either.

At this moment, he had a mental picture of babies without mothers, toddlers without parents, school children alone and unprotected in a world which had gone insane.

What could he do? He could perhaps go into the city and pick up a dozen or so. A dozen out of all those millions—dear God!

He shifted uncomfortably. It was going to worry him like hell from now on.

He would have liked to forget it. He would have liked to shrug it aside, wash his mental hands of it, on the quite justifiable grounds that the problem was insoluble.

He *knew* it was insoluble but the realization was not going to lift the weight from his mind or wash away the mental pictures.

He lit yet another cigarette, scowling. You were the way you were, you cared about things or you didn't. It was a fine thing when you could kill a seagull by a mere whim but couldn't help—.

His thoughts came to an abrupt stop.

*Who said he couldn't?*

If some bloody nut case could ship three luxury cars

out of a showroom, he, Travers, could have a try at saving a few hundred kids.

He picked up his order book again and, as he did so, a picture of Beasly came suddenly to his mind.

Beasly was—had been—his area sales manager. It had been his habit, every month, to give a pep talk to the salesmen.

Travers had always listened with half an ear, his thoughts elsewhere, usually on women, but some words had stuck.

'When you set out to make sales, gentlemen, don't think in terms of two or three sales a day, multiply that number by ten. Twenty orders, thirty orders, don't limit yourselves, *think big*—.'

Think big, that was it, why only a hundred children?

He began to scribble in his order book but nearly an hour had passed before he was satisfied.

*At this moment, countless human infants and children are hungry, frightened and probably without love, warmth and shelter. They are not protected from the dangers which the present situation has brought into being.*

*I command that these same children are, from hereon, loved, fed, clothed, housed and protected against all present dangers. Further, that they be given the necessary education for survival in the present situation.*

He read it through four times. Then he read it aloud, prefixing the command word.

The personal results of his efforts, he found startling. The mental pictures with accompanying distress immediately vanished and were replaced by a sense of—what was it? Peace? No not quite peace as he understood it nor was it the smug self-satisfaction of a conscience-salving prayer. Travers cherished a secret and withering contempt for that kind of mentality. No, the feeling was—yes—that was it—it was *assurance*.

It was as if something had tapped him mentally on the shoulder and told him the matter was being taken care of.

He felt a shiver of unease inside him. *What* was taking care of it?

This was the hell of a frightening world and he could say that again many times.

He glanced at his watch. Ten past three, about time he got out of here and took a look at the city. He might make it if he kept to minor roads.

He switched on and glanced at the dials. Hell! Less than a gallon, he'd never make the city on that.

Uneasily, feeling that he was robbing some unfortunate garage owner, he commanded a full tank.

The needle swung round to 'full' almost immediately but he felt no satisfaction. It was all too damned easy, wasn't it? As he saw it, that was one hell of a big danger, you could become *dependent* on tricks like that.

He would have to keep a firm grip on himself, it would be too easy to give way. Absolute power corrupts and, with the minimum of encouragement, lead to insanity. Before you knew where you where, you were like Alcott, deluding yourself you were God.

Further, you couldn't have everything you wanted without some sort or repercussion, could you? What was taken had to be replaced. Those who kept taking would, sooner or later, be presented with an account.

Travers put the car into 'drive' and eased back onto the

dirt road. Fifteen miles an hour was going to be the absolute maximum. One could never tell what might be round the next bend.

Aloud he said suddenly. 'Of all the bloody fools.' He had forgotten the radio. He switched it on. The dial lit but there was no sound. He tried all the bands without success. Radio-wise, not a single station in this part of Canada was on the air.

He sighed. More than ever, it looked like the end of the world.

He drove on, keeping a careful watch. Near the end of the dirt road, he came upon four cars, all empty, and a truck which had careened into a tree.

A mile further on, two cars had collided. A body lay in the road, an elderly man who was gruesomely dead.

As he drove on, crashed or abandoned cars became more frequent. He realized he would never make the city in daylight and attempting it in the dark seemed like pointless suicide.

He managed a turn with a good deal of shunting in the narrow road and, as he did so, he noticed a small general store on his right.

On impulse, he pulled up and went inside. No one came to serve him and the place had the same feeling of desolation as the inn.

As yet, no looters had run riot. The till was open, coins and notes lay untouched.

Travers made a selection, taking careful note of the prices. Eight cans of beans, coffee, bread still reasonably fresh, chocolate. Then with some foresight, a cooking stove and fuel.

He took his load to the car and went back for more. More cans of food, a sleeping bag and a ground sheet.

In the rear rooms he found a shotgun and after a brief search, two boxes of shells.

He carefully listed the items, wrote an explanatory note which he placed in the till with the necessary cash. After all, the owner might return. Perhaps it was a quixotic gesture, he was well aware he could have obtained all the items by an effort of will but somehow this was doing things the right way.

He drove back to the dirt road and after driving about three miles selected a spot between two tall trees. A low cliff was behind him protecting his back while the trees concealed him from the air.

He cooked himself a meal and ate hungrily. By the time he had finished, the autumn dusk was closing in.

He spread the ground sheet, climbed into the sleeping bag and, with the shotgun within finger-reach, fell into a dreamless sleep.

He awoke about midnight under a startlingly clear sky. There was no moon but the stars were myriad and brilliant.

The visible horizon, in the direction of the city, still glowed sullenly red. It was clear that major fires were still raging in several districts.

Far behind him, invisible because of the low cliffs, something passed across the sky with a curious whispering sound. For several seconds the tips of the surrounding trees were lit by a flickering but intensely brilliant blue-green light.

Travers wondered if it was the disc thing but doubted

it, that had been predominantly red. What the hell, then, was this?

It was then that a twig snapped a bare ten feet away and his fingers closed convulsively on the shotgun.

As silently as possible he began to draw it towards him and, at the same time, point it in the direction of the sound.

'If you attempt to lift that thing,' said a low cultured voice, 'I shall be compelled to blow your damned head off. Take it easy, Mr Travers, I come as a friend.'

Travers said, wearily. 'Seems I don't have much choice. Right, it's your move.'

'Sensible, sensible. Pick up your torch and take a look at me.'

Travers did so and saw a tall well dressed negro.

'I am not a nut, Mr Travers, as I said, I come as a friend. Certain people of all nations impose upon themselves principles from which they refuse to depart. You were clearly one of these people, hence my visit.'

'Thank you for the compliment.' Travers was still guarded. 'Just where did you get my name?'

'There are enough documents in your car to furnish me with that. However, I will be frank. Like yourself, I have faculties—some you have yet to discover for yourself.'

'So what do you want with me?'

'Not I alone—we. There are only a handful of us yet but we're collecting others like us.'

The negro came forward and, in the light of the torch, laid an automatic on the edge of the ground sheet.

'Will you accept this as gesture of goodwill?'

Grudgingly Travers laid his shotgun beside it. 'OK, what now?'

'We want you to join us.'

'For what reason, Mr—?'

'Robinson, Dave Robinson. As to the reasons, Mr Travers, survival should be reason enough. As you must have noted, new laws have come into operation and civilization, as we know it, has ceased to exist.'

'Where are this—er—handful?'

'I brought a map. If you will hold the torch a little closer, please—thank you. We are here, you see I've marked it. It is only eighty miles in a direct line but a hundred and twenty if you avoid the towns which would be advisable under the circumstances.'

Robinson paused. 'It may occur to you to teleport yourself there but I advise against it. One needs a clear mental picture of the area and one tiny mistake—. We are in a summer hotel, poised picturesquely on a cliff edge. You see the danger?'

Travers did and shivered slightly. 'I guess a good many have gone in this business.'

'Too many. I know of several who wished themselves elsewhere. To my knowledge none have returned. The human race has been presented with, or had foisted upon it, a power over which it has no control. It appears to be a wholly impersonal power which obeys one's slightest whim, too often with fatal results.

'One could say, without stretching credulity too far, that we have contracted a parapsychic disease. Some, you included, have gained a measure of control which is yet another reason for you to join us. The preservation of the entire race may depend on people like ourselves.'

Robinson rose. 'I'll leave the map. See you when you arrive—good luck.'

Abruptly he disappeared.

Travers sat staring at the place where he had stood, then reached for the map. He was strangely unsurprised. Maybe he was numb or maybe you could become used to almost anything.

He began to think about the proposition. There was a lot of sense in what the man had said but, more immediately, it provided an objective. It gave him somewhere to *go* where at least there must be rational people.

He studied the map. With luck, he could drive a fair part of the way if he kept to minor roads. Trouble was, he would have to cross the highway which would not only be unpleasant but dicey. That alien disc might be hanging around—why had he forgotten to ask Robinson about the aliens?

He shrugged. It would have to wait until he got there —if he got there. Somewhere along the route he would have to leave the car and continue on foot. Oh hell, worry about that later, get himself a meal, he was no longer sleepy anyway.

He was on the move an hour before dawn but it was not an uneventful journey.

Just after first light, someone took a shot at the car and the bullet passed through a rear window.

An hour later a demented woman with wildly disordered hair ran out of a farm house and threw a brick at the car.

Ten miles further on, in quiet woodland, the road was blocked by a mass of shimmering strands.

Travers recalled that he had already met one spider, he was not keen on meeting another.

It meant yet another detour and by noon, he figured he had driven sixty miles which, in the final reckoning, had brought him only ten miles closer to his destination.

He decided to stop and have a meal. When the time came for him to go on on foot, he'd need all his strength.

He pulled in beside a small lake, careful to park beneath some trees.

In the middle of the meal, he saw the cat and made a grab for the shotgun.

Normally he would have thought 'cat' and dismissed it from his mind.

This cat, however, was different. In the first place, it was bright green and, in the second, it was walking on the water.

## CHAPTER THREE

He wondered briefly if he was hallucinating and decided it was an unhappy explanation. He preferred a real cat, however bizarre. He had enough to worry about without the added burden of hallucinatory images.

The cat seemed to become aware of his intense stare and turned towards him.

Travers hooked his finger round the trigger. A bright green cat might be harmless and it might not.

As it drew closer and the water shallower he saw that it had not been actually walking on the surface of the water. The green fur extended the normal distance down the legs but, below this were yellow—stilts? No, not stilts but a continuation of the legs but no longer furry. The creature had thin yellow legs below the fur like those of storks, herons and similar long-legged wading birds.

Again, it was not quite a cat. There was a bright tuft of green fur, rising like a stiff tassel between the ears. The eyes were round and golden.

It struck him suddenly that the cat was frightened and was coming to him because it needed help. He could not explain what evoked the thought but the realization seemed to establish a rapport between himself and the animal.

The cat was not only frightened, it was hungry. It was used to eating—there was no word—but he had a mental picture of a yellowish plant, vaguely resembling mimosa, which grew on the surface of the water. At the same moment, he had a mental picture, so vivid, it was almost frightening.

He saw a huge lake, covered with great patches of the yellow plant. Surrounding the lake were slender silver-coloured trees. Above the lake, a huge greenish sun blazed down from a sky which was not blue but purple.

The picture vanished as quickly as it had come and he saw that the creature was now clear of the water. It lifted the long slender legs delicately and carefully like a bird.

He thought; 'a vegetarian cat and for some reason it likes me.'

Aloud, he said: 'I don't know what I can do to help.' But he did, almost before the sentence was complete.

*'Aufmachen. I wish this creature was back where it came from.'*

There was no time to blink, the creature simply snapped out of visible existence. There was a faint rush of wind as if the surrounding air had rushed in to occupy the space it had left.

Half an hour later he was on his way, but a few hundred yards from the highway he knew he must leave the car. He did so with regret. Like all good drivers he had become emotionally attached to it.

He filled his rucksack to capacity, tied on his ground sheet and sleeping bag and started off.

He skirted a truck which not only completely blocked the road but had spilled its load of vegetables in all directions.

Beyond was an overturned car and, beyond that, more overturned and wrecked vehicles. It was evident by the smell which reached him that many still contained bodies. If it was like this on a normal road, what would it be like on the major highway far ahead?

He had been walking less than twenty minutes when a fountain of violet fire leapt from the ground a bare ten feet away.

He flung himself flat and a rush of searing heat passed above him, searing the leaves of some nearby trees.

Travers had seen action in war and the old instincts fell immediately into place.

He rolled into a convenient hollow and began to inch his way forward to the cover of a small woodland on his right.

Instinct, or the reflexes of experience, had locked his hand on the shotgun and he made sure he had it in a position to fire.

Another fount of violet fire leapt upwards but it was well behind him. It struck him that his attacker, or attackers, had lost him and were guessing at his position. On the other hand they might be trying to flush him out. In which case, there would be a series of shots in the hope that his nerve would break, that he would rise, exposing himself.

The second guess was the correct one. There were six 'shots' in the immediate vicinity before he reached the cover of the trees.

Once in them, he leapt to his feet and ran but the thought that he had made cover must have occurred to his attackers also.

Before he had covered twenty feet, there was the familiar 'swooshing' sound. A tangle of blazing branches come crashing down behind him.

He saw that at least three trees had been shorn off and had actually crowned in a brief swirl of flame.

He began to zigzag between the trees but in a rough arc which he hoped would take him back in the direction from which the shots were coming.

Trees continued to explode in flame but he could tell that the marksman was following a straight line.

When the trees began to thin, he dropped flat and began to pull himself forward by his elbows. All the time he was watching, the shotgun ready in his hands.

The ground ahead was undulating, with a few sparse trees, bushes and a few slender saplings.

Travers acknowledged to himself that he was both

frightened and angry. At the moment, however, anger over-rode fear. What did they think he was—some damned animal to be hunted down?

He eased himself a little further forward and something caught his eye. In a depression between a small group of saplings and an uneven mass of hawthorn was the top of a small blue delivery van.

Its presence had barely registered when there was a stab of violet light just in front of the van followed, almost immediately by a distant crashing of branches.

Travers studied the terrain with an experienced eye. He had been on more patrols than he cared to remember during the war and a lot of lessons had stuck.

There was a small stream quite close to him which had carved for itself a natural ditch. If he kept on his belly, he might make the stream without being seen. Once there, he could make it on hands and knees to within twenty feet of the thing which stabbed violet.

He realized that for any hope of success, he must put the thought of all things alien out of his mind. That kind of idea would undermine his nerve and affect his judgement. No, go back a few years, this was an enemy machine gun nest which had to be knocked out—pity he hadn't a couple of grenades.

He placed his rucksack carefully in a hollow, then slid on his belly into the stream.

It was only an inch or so deep. He made it to the point he wanted and raised himself cautiously.

Violet stabbed from behind a small grassy mound and the distant crashing of branches assured him that his attacker had no idea he was so close.

He found a big stone, threw it high in the air and waited.

There was a satisfying clang as it struck the roof of the van.

Travers stood up and fired both barrels.

The first shot took the top off the mound in a shower of earth, the second knocked a hole in the side of the van as big as a dinner plate.

Travers shouted: 'Give in, you're surrounded!' Then he sprinted twenty feet in a crouching position.

'Don't shoot! For God's sake, don't shoot!' The voice was human, male and terrified.

'Throw down your arms and come out in the open with your hands raised. Any funny business and my partner will toss a grenade right behind you.'

'I hear you, I'm coming—don't shoot, please.'

Travers, re-loading quickly, saw raised hands appear above the level of the hollow. A face followed and a tall thin body in blue jeans.

'Come over here, very slowly and very easily.'

Reaction was setting in and Travers found the gun shaking a little in his hands. He was grateful that the weapon had a normal pull instead of a hair-trigger.

'Any others?' Tension made Travers' voice unnaturally harsh.

'No—no—honest.' A youth came towards him, obviously terrified. He had an adenoidal, sloppy sort of face and vacuous blue eyes. Travers guessed his age as around seventeen.

'I hope it is honest because you're going to walk back and I'm going to follow. This gun will be a foot from your back. If I have to fire it, it will blow you nearly in half.'

'There's no one else.' The youth's voice broke, he was clearly on the verge of tears.

They walked down a slight incline to a small hollow. In it was the blue van. Written on the side was; MARPLES LTD. DAIRY PRODUCE. It was crammed to the roof with tinned foods, guns and a large box of obviously looted jewellery.

Beside the van was a tent, a folding canvas chair, a camp stove and the remains of a meal on a large coloured plate.

Half way up the slope down which they had just descended was a curiously shaped tube of a black but oddly glittering substance.

Travers, gun still pointed, indicated the tube.

'Is that what you were using?'

'You ain't going to hurt me?'

'Answer my question, blast you.'

'Yes, sir, that's it, but—.'

'Shut up! What is it?'

'It's—it's—.' The youth swallowed, his prominent Adam's apple rising and falling as he did so. 'It's a death-ray, sir.'

'A what!'

'A death-ray, sir, honest.'

Travers did not ask where it had come from, the answer was obvious. This damn fool kid had wished for a death-ray and got it.

'What were you firing it at me for?'

'I thought you were one of them things, one of them aliens, honest to God.'

'What aliens?'

'Ain't you seen 'em? They got all of Alsone Valley tied up tight. The 'ole place is packed with funny-looking green buildings.'

'Alsone Valley?' Travers removed the map from his breast pocket. 'Point it out to me—we're just here.'

'Well, there's Alsone Valley, there.'

Travers scowled and thought 'it would be'. The valley lay directly across his route. It would mean, at a rough estimate, an additional hundred and twenty miles. He'd planned to cut straight across the valley to avoid Willerton, a small industrial town.

'What are these aliens like?'

'What I seen, like thick poles, maybe eight feet tall. They keep changing colour like they was lit from inside and they got a lot of thin green arms.'

'And I look like that?' Travers was angry again.

'Something moved, sir, I didn't know it was you and I was scared, see? I thought everyone but me was dead.'

'Well make bloody sure next time. You came damn near to having your fool head blown off.'

'I wouldn't have shot at a human, honest, sir. I got this death ray, see? I reckoned that would stop the bastards.' Travers saw that the youth was telling the truth and lowered himself wearily into the canvas chair.

'You like a nice cup of coffee, sir, or I got some tea around somewhere?' The youth was anxious to show his sincerity. 'Name's Tom—Tom Beamish.'

He pointed to the van. 'Did deliveries with that once. Dunno what 'appened to the boss, Mr Chester, 'ole place was wrecked when I went in.'

Travers nodded understandingly, then something attracted his attention.

'What happened to your hand?'

'Dunno.' Beamish studied his right hand, frowning. 'Thought it was dirty at first but the black wouldn't wash off. Don't hurt or nothing, works orlright. Funny, ain't it?'

Travers didn't think it was funny. The youth's hand was coal black and covered in protuberances like huge warts.

Realization struck him suddenly. 'Have you been using your—er—death-ray with that hand?'

'Why, yes, what's that got to do with it?'

'I don't know.' Travers rose, crossed over to the black tube and studied it without touching it. As he bent closer, he felt a tingling sensation in his face and drew back hastily.

The tube was radiating something and, more obvious still, it had never been designed for a human hand. There was no butt and only an oddly recessed stud for the firing mechanism. Beamish must have found it extremely difficult to insert his finger in the recess.

Glancing again at the blackened hand, Travers knew that the organic entity which had built the weapon was wildly unhuman. Possibly the radiation, or whatever it was that the weapon gave off, had no effect on the thing which used it. Just as, for example, the acrid smoke from a shotgun had no effect on the human user. To another life-form, however, the fumes of burnt cordite might prove instantly or accumulatively lethal.

He straightened. 'I'd leave that thing alone if I were you.'

Beamish nodded. 'Reckon I will unless I'm sure it's them aliens. I got guns in the van. There's an automatic thing, dead soldier 'ad it but I don't know 'ow to work it.'

'Show it to me.'

The youth retrieved it from a pile of canned food with some effort.

Travers glanced at it. 'Oh, a Bren. This the only clip?'

'All there was with it.'

'Its full but don't waste it. When you've shot this lot off, you've had it—understand?'

Travers showed him how to operate the weapon and wished him luck. He had the certain feeling, however, that Beamish would not be around long enough to worry about an attack. Unless he was very much mistaken, the blackness affecting the hand had already reached the shoulder.

The youth's movements were jerky and occasionally he staggered. It was, perhaps, merciful that he appeared not to realize it himself.

'You ain't going?'

'Sorry, I must. I have some friends to meet.'

'I'll come with you.'

'As you wish, but I have to go right round the valley.'

'Oh—oh—well, no. Them aliens is all over the place, they scare me.'

Ten minutes later, Travers was on his way again. He walked slowly, already weary. How long since he had taken a walk of more than two miles, if that?

When he reached the major highway, he crossed it with considerable caution. He had to watch both the ground and the sky above him.

Not all the vehicles were wrecks he noticed. Some had

been abandoned without panic and were carefully locked. Others just stood there, doors hanging open.

Four contained dead men, one a dead woman and he almost ran down the grass bank on the opposite side of the highway.

He admitted to himself, that crossing the highway had proved more unnerving than he had expected. To him there had been something ghostly about the utterly silent road packed with unmoving vehicles. The familiar names on the various models somehow made it worse.

Then there was the little doll or nodding dog in the rear window and the pseudo-comic notices on the backs of the sportier models.

*If you can read this you're too damn close* was one example he noticed.

*People* had driven these cars. Business men, would-be holiday makers with families, crooks, illicit lovers.

Where were they all? Surely not all of them had vanished from the face of the earth?

Travers was afflicted with sudden overwhelming loneliness and a sense of desolation.

There were, of course, many signs of panic on both sides of the highway.

Suitcases, some open and spilling their contents onto the grass. Women's handbags, fragments of clothing hanging from branches and thorns.

Perhaps the alien disc thing had suddenly appeared above. On the other hand, he thought, wearily, there could be another explanation. It only needed a dozen or so drivers to wish themselves elsewhere—.

He saw the picture in his mind. A glance in the mirror,

a more powerful car overtaking. Another glance, the car was still overtaking but the driver had vanished. God! The car ahead was empty too.

It was a situation which would undermine the nerve of the strongest man, particularly so with pile-ups happening all around.

Travers sighed and trudged on. The world, his world, had come to an end. Worse, age-old laws had been overruled. Man could defy gravity, space and time and the powers of life and death resided in the whim of the individual.

He stepped over a low hedge and found an automatic weapon pointing straight at his head.

'Drop the shotgun, friend.'

He obeyed, there was no choice.

He saw that there were two men. The first was a private soldier, the second was in civilian clothes but wore a white arm band.

The soldier said: 'You are in a military area. Raise your hands above your head and walk ahead.'

He shrugged and, after a few minutes walking, found himself looking down a long grassy slope to lower ground.

On the level plain below was, presumably, the armed might of the immediate district.

There were seventy or so military trucks, a sprinkling of light tanks, a rocket launcher and an ancient and rusty-looking howitzer.

Among the conglomerate of transport—none of it dispersed—were several caravans, their bright colours contrasting oddly with the trucks about them. From one of the caravans, a huge and vivid flag fluttered limply.

Why don't they write 'Command' on the roof thought Travers sourly. What damn fool would advertize his presence with a flag like that? Certainly no experienced soldier.

He realized they were guiding him towards the caravan with the flag.

'The Master will want to question you personally,' said the soldier.

Travers thought; another nut and a civilian nut at that.

In the distance, to his right and beyond the transport, men were drilling or going through the motions of attack.

To his left, again beyond the transport, were a large number of tents of various colours and sizes. They were packed so closely together that they were a virtual death-trap.

One good gun crew or strafing aircraft could bring about a shambles from which this little lot would never recover.

The soldier stopped short of the caravan and addressed a guard at the door.

'Civilian picked up, sector eight.'

'Right, I'll see—' The guard put his head just inside the door for some seconds and then withdrew it. 'Conduct the prisoner in.'

The Master sat behind a paper-littered desk which was much too big for the caravan.

'Name, age and recent profession?'

Travers told him but he made no attempt to write down the answers.

He said: 'True so far, but how far? Where were you going?'

'To meet some friends.'

'What friends?'

Before Travers could answer, he said: 'Ah, I get the picture, another group of funk-specialists hiding out in the mountains until the trouble blows over—they hope.'

Travers frowned. Where the hell was the man getting his information? The answer came to his mind almost before he had asked himself the question and he took immediate counter measures.

*Aufmachen. I command that it be impossible for any man or woman to read my mind without my consent.*

He saw that the 'Master' was busily writing a series of questions and studied him covertly. He was a thin man, pink faced, with a mane of crinkly greying hair.

Travers decided that if he was not a nut, he was damn near it, a borderline case. There was something about his movements and a feeling of intensity which suggested he was a fanatic.

'Where, precisely, are your friends in the mountains?'

Travers said nothing and the other looked up quickly, his mouth a compressed line.

'Ah! So we have a clever one here.'

Travers said: 'Pardon?' With just the right ingredients of surprise and mock innocence to make it insulting.

The thin face flushed. 'I have met your sort before, Travers, but I advise against a vanishing act. Too many have teleported themselves into lethal situations.'

He paused and appeared to be thinking deeply. Then he said: 'Before you shut me out, I probed around enough to discover that you were intelligent. I will give you something not given to all who see me. I will give you a chance.'

He motioned briefly to a small wooden chair. 'Sit down. How much do you know?'

'Not a lot. A large number of people, maybe all, have become parapsychic and don't know how to handle their powers. I have seen what I assume to be an alien vessel and I have been told that there are aliens around.'

The other nodded, reached into one of the desk drawers and produced some photographs.

'Take a look at these.'

Travers did so. The prints were a little hazy, had obviously been taken with a telescopic lens but they showed long lines of curiously architectured buildings faintly resembling bungalows. Here and there were pillar-like objects which might have been the things described by Beamish.

'Alien settlement,' said the Master. 'How do you like the idea?'

'I don't, naturally.'

'Naturally, you say, what are you prepared to do about it?'

'Such as?'

'You could join me. I am building an army here. Every day, twenty or thirty refugees come in, we're growing fast. My aim is to cleanse the earth of aliens forever.'

'With that shambles?' Travers was unable to keep the contempt out of his voice.

Oddly, the other did not seem to resent it. 'I know, under normal conditions, my force is a sitting duck for orthodox attack but, at the moment, there is a state of impasse. The aliens have the barrier—a sort of defensive screen—through which we cannot pass. On the other hand, I have erected a canopy of mental force above this encampment which nothing can penetrate.'

'I understand you,' said Travers in a flat voice. His mind was elsewhere and seemed to be working with peculiar clarity.

'A mental canopy through which nothing could penetrate.' There seemed to be a flaw somewhere and he knew instantly what it was. 'Nothing, meant anything which the human imagination could conceive and there was the danger spot. No doubt the man had thought of missiles, organic bodies, radiation and various lethal rays which he would probably visualize as light beams. As such, it was, no doubt effective but what about *the forms of attack which the human imagination could not conceive*?

They were facing aliens and, with this in mind, the alleged canopy could well prove just about as effective as chicken wire against a tropical storm.

He said: 'Suppose I refuse to join you?'

The other shrugged. 'Oh, you'll join me, Travers, you'll be conscripted and assigned to special duties. You'll go into the Cats-paw troop which will give you a taste of alien technology.'

He paused and smiled thinly. 'You see, we want to know the extent of the alien barrier and the only way to do this is to send a man into it. We use rebels and malcontents like yourself for this job. Encouraged by skilled marksmen who have orders to shoot dead those who attempt to escape, you will walk forward until the barrier stops you.'

'If you survive the impact—a few have—you will then try again at another spot. It is, you see, essential for us to know both the strength and extent of the barrier before we attack.'

# CHAPTER FOUR

'And if I join you?'

'You will be clothed, fed, housed and kept in training until the day of attack.'

'Presumably that will only come about if, and when, you discover how to penetrate this alien barrier.'

The Master didn't like that, Travers could see it, but he said, evenly: 'A question of time. Time to build up our reserves, armour and weapons. When I am ready, I shall unleash forces which will stagger the imagination. The aliens will be swept from the earth in one great action, man will reclaim his birthright.'

Travers said nothing, aware that his expression reflected no corresponding zeal or enthusiasm.

'The aliens will have weapons, too,' he observed, drily.

'I am not a fool, my friend, you forget I can call upon the knowledge of the universe.'

Again Travers' mind seemed to be working with unusual clarity.

'There are limits to that, too, you know. You can only bring to yourself the weapons which your imagination can conceive. Weapons of greater sophistication which, we assume, must exist in the universe, would be useless.'

'I don't understand you.' The Master's face was pale now and the corner of his mouth twitched.

'It seems simple enough to me. Suppose you and your army had only reached the bow-and-arrow conception of warfare. Tell me, of what use would be the introduction of a machine gun? Would you know how to load it, aim it and fire it? My guess is that you would toss it aside as useless or employ it as a club. A box of grenades should prove even more interesting and, with weapons like this, who needs an enemy?'

The Master rose, eyes protruding and a blue vein standing out on his left temple.

'You cock-a-hoop intellectual son of a bitch.' He banged his clenched fist hysterically on the top of his desk. 'Guard! Guard!'

The guard entered. 'Master?'

'Conduct this intellectual excrement to Sergeant Warren. He is to lead, *lead*, you understand, the squad into the barrier.'

The guard grasped Travers' arm. 'Yes, Master—come on, you.'

Travers was conducted by two armed guards to a point well clear of the camp.

There was a sergeant with a submachine gun and two hard-looking men with rifles.

On the ground, three unshaven and dejected-looking men lay sprawled.

One of the men looked up at Travers tiredly. 'Welcome to the suicide squad. Pray, if you can pray, for a first time hit. Dave, over there—' he indicated one of the sprawling men—'is tough. He's walked into that bloody thing five times.'

He removed a stub of cigarette from behind his ear and lit it.

'Ever been hit by a barbed wire fist, chum? That's what it's like, you don't see no lacerations but it's hell. In the end a burst of fire is preferable to trying it again.'

'Don't tell him about it, Pearce,' said the sergeant. 'He is just going to find out for himself, one man job. Get moving, you and listen. You walk straight towards that first tree, there. About ten feet past it, you'll hit the barrier. Remember, our guns will be centred in the middle of your back and we have orders to shoot if you try anything. Now get going.'

Travers walked forwards, acutely conscious of the weapons behind him.

He reached the tree. He saw that there were more trees beyond which gradually thickened. Ahead he recalled from the map, was the valley and he was approaching the narrowest point. He found it bitterly ironic that he should be following his chosen route with guns at his back.

It was then that he saw the body. It lay contorted on the grass, one arm half raised as if to defend itself.

Unconsciously he slowed his pace, he must be within a foot or so of the damn barrier.

'Keep moving, you!'

There was a report and a bullet slapped into the ground a few feet behind him.

'The next one will be between your shoulder blades.'

He stepped past the body and went forward. His skin

felt dry yet perspiration was crawling down his body in streams. Any moment now and a thing like a barbed wire fist would strike at that part of his body which touched it first.

Shakily he continued to walk forward but poised to spring back. Where was the damn thing? Why couldn't he hit the bloody barrier and get it over?

There were shouts behind him.

'Where's the bastard going?'

'He must be through it!'

Before the implications of the words sank into his mind, there was a long savage burst of machine gun fire.

Desperately he tried to fling himself flat, knowing it was too late.

As he went down, a number of pink splashes appeared in mid-air just short of his falling body.

As he struck the ground, there was another burst of fire and several single shots.

Again the pink splashes.

'My God,' he thought. 'I'm through the barrier and it stops bullets.'

He began to crawl forward to the thickening trees, then realized the absurdity of crawling.

He rose and began to walk forwards unsteadily, his body shaking from released tension.

There was firing behind him and a plopping sound which might have been a mortar but he didn't look back.

Ten minutes later he saw the alien and, strangely, it caused him no alarm.

It was almost as Beamish had described it, save that it reminded him of a giant cactus. It was lit interiorly with a softly changing light.

When he first saw it, it was predominantly pink but it changed to an intense and beautiful blue as he approached.

*'Welcome.'*

He came to a dead stop. The word had sort of appeared in his mind with a marked feeling of friendliness and sincerity.

What the hell! Nothing should be able to get into his mind.

He received a faint feeling of amusement. *'Apologies, but only a few hours ago you did specify no man or woman and I am neither.'*

He found himself responding to the amusement for the statement was wholly true.

He thought suddenly: 'this is an alien, why am I not afraid of it? It kills people, indirectly, that barrier—.'

*'It failed to kill you, Mr Travers. The barrier, as you call it, is, you see, selective. You must understand that it is not there to protect us but our charges. Those the barrier decides are dangerous to our charges, it repels painfully but it admits those who favour their well-being.'*

The answer was a complete puzzle to Travers but he still felt no fear. The alien felt—yes, that was the word—felt completely benevolent.

*'I am here to conduct you across the settlement—this way.'*

It moved and he saw that its base—was that the right word?—was supported by hundreds of hair-like tentacles on which it moved quite swiftly.

Travers was puzzled, both by himself and the situation. He ought to hate this thing, it had established a settlement on Earth. In brutal fact, it was an invader.

*'I am not an invader.'*

'But you're an alien, you don't belong here.'

*'Let us correct the perspective. I am an alien but I am not an invader.'*

'Then what the hell are you?'

*'I am a guest.'*

'A what!' Travers tried to put force into the exclamation but somehow failed. 'Who invited you?'

*'You did for one. It is why you are welcome here.'*

'I? For God's sake!'

*'It is true. You and many hundreds of thousands of others. You will understand in a very short time.'*

Travers realized that they were now descending a long green slope to the valley and the valley was filled with curiously architectured buildings. As the Master's photographs had shown, they were bungalow-size but there the resemblance to anything earthly stopped.

In the first place they were a complete contradiction. They were dull green in colour but managed to look bright and cheerful. Somehow they succeeded in blending a curve with an acute angle and achieving an artistic effect.

Sounds reached him, familiar, and despite its short absence, nostalgic sounds—children!

'What's going on?'

*'Come.'*

He followed, half angry and wholly confused.

He saw that each building was a separate unit with an area of grass between each and, in the open streets, children played. Apparently and amazingly, *happy children.*

There were numerous aliens standing around but the children seemed quite untroubled by them.

Then an amazing thing happened. A small boy approached one of the aliens: 'Can I go fishing tomorrow, Dad?'

Travers did not hear a reply but the small boy smiled and said: 'Reckon it'll keep fine for that, eh?'

*'I am being a little unfair to you, please close your eyes and open them again.'*

Travers did so and was a little staggered at the change. The buildings were still there, the children, but in place of the aliens were, apparently, wholly normal men and women.

The alien at his side had become a ruddy-faced man in a brightly coloured shirt. Not far away, an exquisite Japanese girl led two little girls—replicas of herself—by the hand. A dark haired man was playing ball with two small boys—.

'I don't get it.'

*'You are seeing us as the children see us.'*

'Maybe I'm stupid but why?'

*'Their parents are dead. We are telepaths and when they look at us we make sure they see their parents.'*

'You mean you're here to *help*? You're here to look after the children? Good God! How did this come about?'

*'It is a simple explanation. When you, and many thousands of others, sought help for the children, the forces which your race now control made our advent possible. Since we can read minds, we know the physical and emotional needs of your young. All of them, with a few exceptions from institutions, believe themselves to be living in normal conditions with familiar parents or guardians.'*

Travers said: 'Why? Why should you? At the risk of

sounding cynical and ungrateful, what's in it for you?'

*'A sensible question. Let us not, therefore, confuse the issue with sentiment. A human philosopher propounded the theory that all men act in self-interest. This included the self-sacrificing as well as the egomaniacs. The same truth applies to all reasoning intelligences. We care for the helpless because our natures are such that we derive pleasure from such work.'*

'And I thought I was cynical.'

*'That is not a sensible observation. Your human nurses derive pleasure in attending the sick otherwise they would shun such a demanding profession. Do not confuse self-interest with selfishness, they are worlds apart. When you fall in love—and you will—you will seek to make your loved one happy because in her happiness you will find your own. A selfish man, however, will seek to derive every possible pleasure from his woman's body without thought for her feelings or needs—you see the difference? Nonetheless, all reasoning intelligences act in self-interest, however much they may seek to convince themselves otherwise. You do, so also, do we.'*

Travers felt chastened and was aware of respect. This thing was a realist and disconcertingly honest. It had made no attempt to impress him with the depths of its compassion or the nobility of its cause. Brutally, such was its nature that it got a kick out of what it was doing and was honest enough to say so.

On the material side, God alone knew how many kids and infants were being housed, fed, clothed and loved by entities they thought were their parents.

*'We have the children of all nations here. In exact*

*figures, fifty-two thousand, eight hundred and four. There are many, many settlements like this one.'*

'Looks like my prayer was answered.'

*'Again, do not confuse the issue. You are in possession of a power which you used for the benefit of others and, to stress a previous point, is it not true, that had you not done so, you would have been inwardly distressed?'*

'Of course I would—I was.'

*'Exactly so. You acted in self-interest.'*

'You make me feel a louse.'

*'On the contrary, you could have dismissed it. You could have sought to acquire power over others. That these, the children, caused you concern reveals a facet of your character which universally would be recognized as 'good' irrespective of motivation.'*

Travers realized that they had left the settlement and were climbing the opposite side of the valley.

'Excuse me, do you have names?'

*'If we meet again, you will recognize me. A telepathic imprint is as recognizable as a human face.'*

'There is so much I want to ask you.'

*'And many of your questions I will not answer. You have been thrust into a position of immense responsibility. With regret, I must tell you that you must gain most of your answers the hard way.'*

The alien stopped. *'We have come to the limits of the settlement.'*

It produced—Travers never discovered quite from where—a small parcel.

*'You have not eaten for a considerable period. These will*

*last you until you reach the village where you will be able to replenish all necessities for your journey.'*

'Well, thank you for all your help, all you are doing and for letting me in.'

*'Please do not thank me for letting you in, thank the barrier. The barrier is both an intelligence and a sentient being. You cannot see it because its form is tenuous and your eyes are not adjusted to perceive its life-rate.'*

The outward man beside Travers became an alien again and extended a thin green tentacle.

*'Your way lies straight ahead but be careful passing through the village.'*

It turned and appeared to Travers to glide away through the grass.

He stepped forward. 'Thanks, barrier,' he said and immediately felt embarrassed. You felt a damned idiot talking to nothing.

Once clear he opened the parcel the alien had given him. He was shocked and amused to find it contained cheese sandwiches. Where the hell had the alien got those?

He ate ravenously and realized, as he finished, that he was tottering from fatigue. No wonder, what with Beamish and all the rest, he must have covered the best part of twenty miles on his two feet.

He found a heap of dry leaves under a tree, fell on them and was asleep almost instantly.

The sun was well up when he awoke and his watch told him it was 9.55.

He had not, as he had hoped, awakened with renewed vigour. He no longer drooped with weariness but he staggered to his feet painfully. He was stiff from head to toe.

'I'll be OK when I've had time to limber up,' he told himself. He didn't believe it. Further, he didn't want to limber up. Every muscle in his body ached and seemed to creak protestingly at the slightest movement.

Faint alarm touched his mind. This was a survival question. If anything horrible came along now, he just hadn't the energy to do damn all about it.

Did he have to feel like this—did he? He wouldn't be taking anything from anyone, would he?

With a suppressed groan he stood upright.

*'Aufmachen, I wish to feel refreshed in mind and body.'*

The result felt like a warm wave which washed through his entire body and mind.

He stretched luxuriously, feeling a strange assurance. He was without ache or pain, he felt fresh and renewed. Get going, eh?

As he walked, he was thinking deeply. There was no need to reason about this. He knew, without knowing how he knew, that there would be no repercussions from this. He had done no more than avail himself of something which was *there*. It was as natural as taking a drink from a mountain stream or utilizing the wind to sail a ship.

Travers had the type of mind which did not permit him to leave the subject there. There had to be limitations, many of which, he recalled having said to the Master. This power, whatever it was, didn't excuse one from thought. In point of fact, it challenged the individual to think harder and think ahead.

As an absurd example, he could command a space ship

and probably get one. There were several factors to consider here. The type of interstellar vessel he had in mind was not constructed by the human race. In which case, it would be an *alien* interstellar vessel and just how would he use an alien space ship? Another unpleasant point was that it might come with its crew. The same crew might take an exceedingly hostile view of the situation. Not that he wanted a space ship, it was just a line of thought to show how damn careful one had to be.

He stopped, took out his map and studied it. About four miles to the village.

He walked on, still thinking. There were others who must also have learned the techniques of survival and not necessarily the good.

The intelligent criminals, the ruthless business men and the power-hungry. The Master had spoken of alien weapons but perhaps he had forgotten that one could 'think' a man dead.

The possibilities were limitless and terrifying. One could think a grenade into a strongpoint and by the same method, pull the pin.

In brief, a ruthless and highly intelligent man could make himself master of the world. His first and most obvious move would be to delete those who were learning quickly enough to stop him.

Travers, walking easily, came to a dead stop. He, himself, was by no means brilliant but he was learning as fast as he could. A rising despot, using his faculties, might learn that he was one who by nature and by principle would oppose him.

It was true that such a man could not wish him dead

directly but there were other ways. A boulder from the top of a cliff for example or a sudden fissure in the earth would close when he fell in it.

Travers sat down on the grass and spent a careful five minutes thinking out a command.

Finally he said, aloud: *'Aufmachen, I wish to be protected against all forms of parapsychic attack, direct and indirect. Further, I command prior warning of hidden danger.'*

The last part of the command had been an afterthought. His presumed despot, when all else failed, might resort to cruder methods—a high powered rifle for example.

He walked on, far easier in mind and, within ten minutes, found himself on a slight rise looking down at the village.

It wasn't much. A small church, possibly of slight historic interest, a few houses lining a narrow street. There was an open green, a filling station and one large building which might be an inn or minor hotel.

There were a few vehicles, at the now familiar odd angles in the streets, but the place appeared deserted.

He descended a slight slope, reached the road and began to approach cautiously.

The road was hedge-lined and, rounding a bend, he came upon an overturned tractor. It had gone into a ditch and what remained of the driver lay pinned underneath.

Travers caught the smell of the decaying body and moved to the other side of the road. War had never inured him to the smell of death.

As he drew nearer the houses, the smell increased and he found himself walking, Indian-like, on his toes. The village was silent—too silent.

The first vehicle he reached had a contorted body in it. The door was open and something caught his eye; beside the body was a rifle.

Holding his breath, he removed the rifle and the three boxes of shells from the passenger seat. The dead man looked as if someone had tied all his muscles in knots before he died.

Travers stepped back and studied the rifle. It was a formidable weapon and looked fully capable of knocking a charging elephant back on its haunches with a single shot.

A few steps further on, two dead men lay behind a car. One still clutched a shotgun, an automatic pistol lay on the ground beside the other.

Travers glanced across the road and saw yet another body draped over a low wall. A heavy revolver still hung from the fingers of the limp hand.

The situation was easy enough to sum up. An attack had been mounted on someone, or something, established in one of the buildings up ahead. Most of the corpses wore ordinary working clothes so, presumably, they had been trying to rid the village of something.

He picked up the automatic and thrust it into his pocket. Then, keeping close to the buildings and all possible cover, he began to move up the street.

He regretted the necessity but the map informed him that to do otherwise meant a fifty mile detour or climbing a mountain.

The feel of the heavy rifle in his hands was only faintly comforting. Something in this village didn't need bullets to stop a man.

As he dodged from cover to cover, he became aware that it was getting darker. He looked up. The sun was still shining but more redly. The light in the street was a curious and unpleasant half-light such as occurs during an eclipse of the sun.

The houses too, seemed to have drawn closer together and he thought he saw something huge and black sweep over the roof tops.

It was then something seemed to click in his mind. Parapsychic attack but this aspect of it was illusory and, although visually disturbing, quite harmless.

He went forward a further twenty feet and, in that brief time, it became almost dark. The sun was a blood-red ball no bigger than an orange.

He ignored it and went on. He had already decided that his target was the inn. Whatever had killed those in the village was up there.

He took two more steps, then, six feet to his right, a fissure opened in the surface of the street and a roaring jet of fire shot upwards.

Before he could take it in, another opened in front of him, then a second and a third. It was clear that someone was trying to incinerate him and couldn't do it.

Gaining assurance, he continued forward. Something black and huge dropped from the sky above him but was stopped abruptly before it reached him. Whatever it was made a shrill whistling sound of pain and fluttered upwards.

Travers took stock of his surroundings and saw that he was now a bare fifty yards from the inn.

He leaned on an abandoned car, lifted the rifle to his shoulder and fired at the largest lower window.

The recoil of the heavy rifle made him stagger but the window fell in and, somewhere inside, there was a splintering of glass and a series of faint impacts.

He concluded that the shot had gone into the bar and several bottles had come crashing down.

He fired twice more, putting one shot through the door and the second through the wall.

The place was only wood and experience told him that the splintering inside must be quite impressive.

It seemed to do the trick for the impression of darkness vanished and the street resumed its normal appearance.

'Don't shoot! Oh, please don't shoot any more.'

He was shocked to hear a woman's voice.

## CHAPTER FIVE

He strode forward and, as he did so, the door opened and a woman appeared. She was not old, perhaps in her late thirties, and she wore a filthy flowered frock. Her eyes were staring and he had no doubt in his mind that she was partly deranged.

'Why didn't you die?' Her voice was shrill and somehow combined utter disbelief and terror. 'Twelve times I wished you dead and you wouldn't burn, blast you, you wouldn't burn.'

She ran her fingers through her disordered blonde hair, then pointed down the street.

'The others died, they tried to kill me but I killed them.'

She laughed shrilly. 'Burn the bloody witch, they said, but I showed them. You see what happened to them down there?'

'I saw them,' he said gently.

Briefly she became rational. 'I'm sorry, nothing against you, thought you'd come to kill me. It was Tom what started it. Him and his bloody promises. He said he'd divorce her and marry me but it was only a lie to get me in bed with him.'

'When I found I had powers, I showed 'em. I killed her, thinking he'd come to me but he picked her up in his arms, weeping, so I killed him too, the lying bastard.'

She became deranged again. 'I'm the witch, see? I can ride across the sky with lightning in me hands. I know, I seen a witch in a movie once and I can do it all—why the hell didn't you die?'

She suddenly leapt at him, hands clawed but he stepped aside.

'Save your energy, you can't kill me.'

She stared at him, panting, then seemed to go limp. 'No, I can't kill you. It's all over isn't it? Nothing works for me, not for long, nothing ever has. Do this, Mary. Do that, Mary. None of the men I've known have cared about me, only used me.'

She put her hands over her face. 'Oh God, I wish—'

Travers knew what she was going to say before she said it and shouted a warning but it was too late.

'Oh God, I wish I was dead.'

She crumpled, it seemed, wearily, struck the ground and rolled over on her side.

Travers looked down at her. In death her face was peaceful and it was clear she had once been almost pretty.

He sighed, went inside the inn, found a travelling rug and returned to cover her body. Burial was out of the question, there were too many dead in this village for one man alone.

At the far end of the street, he found the village store. It was wrecked but not looted. Money lay all over the floor from the overturned till.

He managed to replace all he had lost, including ground sheet, sleeping bag and rucksack. There were ample supplies of canned food and, out the back, chickens scratched. He added a dozen fresh eggs to his supplies.

Twenty minutes later he was on his way but he was still thinking of the dead woman. For a brief period she had controlled forces too powerful for her to understand. He had no doubt she had ridden across the sky, cast spells but, in the end had destroyed herself. How many others had gone the same way, thousands, hundreds of thousands?

How many more had been destroyed by the careless irritable words of others? 'Drop dead!' 'Go to hell!' 'Go and jump off a cliff!' He was certain that very few of these words had been said with intent but the effect would be the same.

Travers figured that the population of earth must have been cut in half.

He stopped and studied the map. At a rough estimate, he had fifty miles to go, mostly uphill and by forest paths. Taking his time, four to six days, providing there were no incidents en route.

He glanced at his watch. Best look out for a place to shack up and prepare a meal. He was hungry and the sun was already low in the sky.

He found a large rock with such a pronounced overhang that it almost formed a cave and decided that it was an ideal spot. The rock would not only protect his back but keep him dry in the event of rain.

He began to prepare a meal and, in the middle of it, while he was crouching, something cold pressed into the back of his neck.

'I don't want to kill you,' said a woman's voice. 'Please don't make me.'

He froze but his mind was racing. How come no warning? Why had his faculties let him down? Reason told him the answer—there was no real danger. The owner of the voice might sound determined but, when it came to the crunch, she was psychologically incapable of killing a man in cold blood.

Travers was basically a kind man and disliked hurting people's feelings. Let her keep her self-respect. He decided to play along for a while.

'What do you want me to do?'

'Back away from your gun, please, but drop the one in your belt—fingers and thumb, no tricks.'

He did so. 'Now what?'

'Stay where you are, I want to try something.'

There was a brief period of silence, then 'I can't read you.'

'I'm sorry, I took precautions against that.'

'You, too?'

'Yes.'

'Have you devised a command word—*don't try turning around.*'

'Yes, and I won't try. What is it you want?'

'It's a survival question, I'm hungry.'

'I have more than enough for two.'

'I see that. On the other hand, I've had dealings with six lunatics and fourteen allegedly sane men. Human duplicity is almost limitless, you know. I can't afford to take chances.'

'You could acquire supplies.'

'I know. The last time put me off. I gave my command without really thinking first. I asked for a plate of bacon and eggs. I got them, stone cold, and the rat on the plate came with them.'

He suppressed an unkind chuckle of amusement. He could imagine the scream, then an idea came to him.

'There's another way.'

'There is?' she sounded dubious.

'Yes, I've never tried it myself but it occurs to me that if you can get things, you might also get answers. For example, am I a nutter, violent or untrustworthy. Perhaps, if you're attractive, you'd better delete the last part.'

'You're refreshingly honest, anyway. Just hold it.'

'I'm inclined that way, although in weak self-justification, I've never forced myself on anyone.'

There was, to him, a rather long period of silence.

Then she said: 'You get a kind of high marks. Okay, you can turn around now.'

He turned. She was, he guessed around twenty-five and she was tiny, almost elfin. The wavy, blue-black hair was uncombed and the large beautiful dark eyes looked tired and strained. There were streaks of mud on the pale, finely boned face and her mouth was full, and to him, inviting.

He pushed the thought hastily out of his mind. This was neither the time nor the place.

His gaze travelled down her. She wore a man's overcoat which reached almost to her ankles and her feet were bare.

'You're a mess,' he said conversationally. 'Come, sit down and I'll fix you something. Sit on the edge of the ground sheet, the grass may be damp.'

A suggestion of a smile touched the corners of her mouth. 'You could use a shave yourself but thank you very much.'

She curled herself, rather than sat, on the edge of the ground sheet.

'I have to be careful, I've nothing on under this coat.'

He broke an egg carefully. 'Try not to cultivate the already flourishing ideas in my mind.'

This time she laughed softly. 'Don't fish, I'm not biting. My name is Lisa, by the way, Lisa Canning.'

She paused and added in a small voice. 'I'm a widow.'

'I'm sorry.'

'Please don't be, he was a bastard.'

'May I ask what happened to him?'

'He killed himself in a way. He said: "may lightning strike me dead if I'm telling a lie!" '

'And it did?'

She nodded slowly. 'Fortunately I didn't have much chance to take it in, next moment I was gone.'

'You wished yourself away?'

'No, apparently a repulsive nut beat me to it. As far as I can gather he wished himself twenty beautiful naked women—I was in the shower, you see.'

She paused then continued. 'As soon as I sized up the situation I—fortunately—only wished myself miles away. I found myself in an empty field and luckily in warm sunshine. I realized something impossible must have happened and started to experiment cautiously. The rest you can probably figure out for yourself.'

'Ready?' He handed her the plate. 'You eat first, only one knife and fork. I wasn't expecting company.'

She began to eat ravenously. 'This is *lovely*. I'm so grateful to you.'

Half way through the meal, she paused. 'I guess I don't look the type, but all the kids have been worrying me. I suppose I sort of prayed for them because I felt better afterwards. You don't happen to have heard anything do you?'

'Yes, I have.' He told her of his own experiences.

'It sounds too incredible to be true but I believe *you*. It's a relief. I love kids but my husband hated them.'

He looked at her empty plate. 'A couple more eggs? Don't let your coffee get cold.'

'Could you spare them? Oh, thank you.'

'About time I introduced myself.' He told her his name and gave her a brief outline of his own experiences.

She looked at him directly. 'You cared about the

children too, basically you must be a very kind man. I have never known a kind man.'

She was quiet for a few seconds. 'Apparently this epidemic only hits people of sixteen and above.'

He took the empty plate and began to cook his own meal in silence. He was irritated to find she attracted him strongly but she was definitely, most definitely not his type. She aroused protective instincts in him and such instincts he regarded as a trap. He preferred independent sensualists who were attracted to him and had no hesitation in showing it. It saved lies—he didn't like lying—or for that matter all the pillow-promises that his kind were prepared to use. As he had often remarked to himself, 'I have principles but no morals.'

He resented the fact that Lisa was playing on his principles but he said, pleasantly enough. 'Any plans—apart from staying alive?'

'None, and you?'

'I'm on my way to join up with some people.'

'You'll take me with you?'

He shook his head and shifted uncomfortably. 'I'm sorry, I can't, I was invited.'

He repeated his brief conversation with Robinson. 'You see, I get the impression they're special and they may not accept you.'

'You could take me along and try.' There were tears in her eyes and inwardly he cursed her for making him feel a heel.

'Look,' he said harshly. 'There are other reasons. I'm no gentleman and I'll try and make you. If I succeed, my conscience will give me hell afterwards because you're not my type. If I fail, I shall spend the rest of the journey trying and slavering. In both cases the association could only lead to friction. It would be better to part now as friends.'

'You exaggerate. I think you're trying to get rid of me gently.'

'I'm not, I swear. I'm an average smoker, I drink moderately but—' He stopped, allowing her imagination to finish the sentence for him.

'I see.' She blinked quickly.

'No, you don't see. What you don't see behind what you call my refreshing honesty, is my personal angle. I'm trying to be honest with myself now as well as you. This is a lead, all you have to do is to comply gracefully but the problems already mentioned remain. I like you and, damn you, you arouse my protective instincts but the women I really favour don't—I make myself plain?'

'I trust my instincts.'

'Well, don't. No one *knows* anyone in this world. They know what the other person chooses to show them, no more. The majority don't even know themselves—'

He stopped, frowning. An idea had occurred to him, an alarming solution but perhaps feasible.

He said, carefully. 'An answer has sort of come to me but you won't like it.'

She looked at him sombrely. 'Since you're intent on stressing how little we know about others, how can you tell? Why not try it for size?'

'True.' There was a growing respect inside him. This woman was no damn fool and she had courage.

'Right, suppose I let you read me. Suppose I—to coin a cliché—bare my soul completely?'

'It sounds reasonable.'

'I haven't finished yet. Would you, in your turn, do the same thing? Would you reveal your entire self without reservations or secret commands?'

She opened her mouth but he waved her quickly to silence. 'Let me finish, please. Don't go blundering into this, only to regret it later. You, for your part, will see—perhaps experience—not only what you consider good but all the bad which exists in every human being. You will do all the mean things I have ever done, experience the jealousies, inner cowardice, sexual phantasies and crude experiences which have gone to make up my life.'

He paused and lit a cigarette. 'It will be far worse for you. You are, I notice, at some pains to conceal your nakedness under that long coat. In contrast, if things go as I expect, dropping that coat will be an easy thing compared to stripping your soul. I shall know everything about you, every secret desire, every animal urge and not one single secret part of you will remain hidden.'

She was silent for a long time, then she said: 'Could you spare me a cigarette, please?'

He lit one and gave it to her without speaking.

She inhaled deeply several times before she spoke. 'If you have guts enough to do it, so have I. It's a deal.'

'You're *sure*?'

'Certain.'

To Travers when he gave the command, the impact was almost shattering. He was not merely in contact with an open mind which concealed nothing, for an immeasurable period of time he *was* Lisa Canning. Her memories were his memories. He knew her cowed mother and overbearing drunken father.

He knew the pains and joys of school days. He shared her first 'crushes' adolescent loves and romantic longings.

He was staggered at the natural passion within her which had never found an outlet. She had unusual self-honesty, above average intelligence, intense feelings and an inexhaustible well of compassion.

She was not all good, he hadn't expected her to be. She was possessive for one thing, sometimes intolerant and distrustful of others.

Travers took the beatings her husband had given her. He felt all the slaps and punches and cringed at the countless public humiliations.

He *lived* those last dreadful minutes before normal civilization fell apart.

He/she was in the shower and Edgar was shouting to make himself heard.

'Listen, when a director takes an interest, you have to be nice to him. You've seen the way he looks at you, can't take his damned eyes off you. If we play it right, I could go up in the world. I could get a seat on the board.

'He pulls the hell of a lot of weight. I've already told him our marriage is modern and he knew what I meant. No need to flaunt the thing, just slip into bed with him a few times discreetly and I'll have him eating out of my hand.'

'Go to hell.'

'Listen you bitch—turn that bloody shower off will you —you have to, understand? I could lose my job.'

'Oh come on!'

'It's true, I swear. May lightning strike me dead if I'm telling a lie.'

He/she saw the sudden livid flash of blue light through the opaque glass of the shower.

He/she caught only a glimpse of the shrivelled smoking body before everything vanished completely.

Travers came to himself feeling a little sick, not with her but her dead husband Edgar. It was true, she had never really known a kind man.

He lit a cigarette and inhaled deeply before he looked at her.

To his surprise, she met his gaze calmly. She did not draw back and there was no revulsion or distaste in her expression.

'You got everything?' he asked uneasily. Maybe something had gone wrong somewhere.

She smiled in a curiously gentle way. 'Don't look so alarmed. Sure I got everything and I mean everything but I judge on what matters to me, on my standards and values. You are a kind man, a sensitive man and I know now that you would never hurt me physically or mentally. Further, it helps to *understand*, do you follow me?'

'Yes, but your understanding doesn't alter my basic nature.'

'So you're strongly sexed and have been badly hurt. A woman who loved you, and you loved in return, could handle you.'

'If she knew how.'

'I know how, someone else could.'

'Someone else would lack your advantages.' He ground out his cigarette. 'In any case, you know what to avoid. Still want to come?'

'Please, but will they accept me?'

'If they don't, they can count me out as well.' He rose. 'It will be dark in half an hour. There's a small stream behind this rock and if you look in my rucksack, there, you'll find soap and a towel. When you come back, you can have the sleeping bag, I'll use the ground sheet.'

She smiled. 'Irrespective of what happened, you would have said that anyway, you're considerate.'

'Get washed woman, you're a mess.'

When darkness fell, he lay on his back for a long time thinking. The mistakes people made. Lisa had married an outwardly charming man to escape the brutality of her father and had landed into something far worse.

He, himself, an orphan, had married an outwardly charming woman who, within a year, had shed her charm. She became shrill, nagging and brazenly unfaithful.

She should have married Edgar, he thought, sourly. He would have become managing director within a year.

God, he was thinking as if the world were the same and it wasn't. Mankind had been reduced to the same level and the managing director was as vulnerable as the office boy. He wondered briefly if many of his colleagues had survived.

He realized with an uneasy feeling, that he was thinking hard about many things to avoid thinking about Lisa.

He had *liked* what he experienced. He liked the warmth, the honesty and the compassion of her personality.

His feelings now had nothing to do with sexual urges

although, he admitted to himself, somehow their potential had increased.

'I could make her happy,' he thought. A bit different to the ex-wife. You could do things for Anne and she would take them in her stride. Sometimes, when in a reasonable mood, she would say 'thanks' indifferently. On the other hand, she had always been quick to find fault, at that she had been brilliant.

Lisa now, she was sensitive, she appreciated consideration, kindness. It would give him a kick just to see her happy—

*'When you fall in love—and you will—you will seek to make your loved one happy because in her happiness you will find your own.'*

Travers went a little cold. What the devil had made him remember that. Blast the alien and his prophecies. In any case, it had no bearing on the present situation, none at all. He was not going to make himself vulnerable again, stick his blasted neck out twice, hell, no.

In any case she was possessive. Uneasily he realized that, a week ago, he would have run a mile at the very suggestion of the word. Now, somehow, the word had been re-interpreted. He'd like Lisa's kind of possessiveness applied to him. No he wouldn't—would he?

Shut up, think of something else or go to sleep. He did neither, for Travers it was the hell of a night.

Lisa herself suffered no such inner turmoil. She liked her experiences and perceived much more, response, compatibility and realization. He was her man and there could be no one else.

She did not dismiss his strong sexual urges but was glad of them. She, herself, had intense feelings and she knew it was a perfect reciprocal match. As for his past, he had conducted himself on a low level because he had been badly hurt and had no wish to make himself vulnerable again.

Her impish humour rose briefly to the surface. 'He won't have the strength to pursue others,' she thought. Not that he would, she knew how to make him want her and keep wanting.

She heard him stir restlessly and smiled half tenderly to herself. He would be reasoning things out now, trying to tell himself that what he was feeling wasn't really true. It was, of course, but her man, being what he was, had to think about it first, she *knew* him. In the end, it would overwhelm him and he'd crack. She hoped it would be soon. She fell into the first dreamless sleep she had experienced for many years.

When dawn came, Travers was haggard and a little irritable. He prepared breakfast in morose silence.

'Have I upset you?' she asked.

He pushed a plate at her. 'No, I'm like this in the mornings.' He managed a smile which was a mockery. 'Well, go on, start eating.'

'I'm waiting,' she said.

'What the hell for?'

She met his scowl with a smile but there was something in her eyes which broke his resolution and he cracked.

'I suppose,' he said harshly. 'You're waiting for me to commit myself. I suppose you're bloody well waiting for me to tell you I love you.'

'Yes, that's it.' She put the plate down and held out her arms to him, her face radiant. 'Yes, my darling, that's it, exactly.'

The sun was high in the sky before they got moving.

'It's a pity there's a slight chill,' he said. 'I prefer you without the coat.'

'You're a dirty old man,' she said.

'I know.' Then, seriously. 'I was Lisa, until I knew you. This wasn't the same—' he paused, searching desperately for words—'it was sort of blessed, on a different level. Oh God, it's so bloody hard to express how I feel.'

'How *we* feel,' she said softly. 'I can't feel a chill.'

'God, you're so beautiful—this is going to be the hell of a long journey.'

'No, we're just going to take a long time covering it. Come here, my love—'

They were within two hundred yards of the hotel when a man stepped from behind a tree with a shotgun.

'Identify yourselves, please.'

'I'm William Travers, I'm expected.'

'By whom?'

'Mr Robinson.'

'Check.' The shotgun lowered. 'What happened? We lost you.'

'Oh, you mean you couldn't contact me. I'm sorry, I had to take safety measures.'

'Reason enough. Robinson will be along in a minute—ah, here he comes now.'

'Good to see you.' They shook hands warmly.

'Who is this woman—' Robinson stopped before he had finished the sentence. 'I'm sorry, fool question, I can feel the relationship but, damn it, this is new. Give me a couple of seconds, please.'

He closed his eyes briefly, then opened them. 'My God, do you two appreciate the situation? Don't tell me you're in love, that shines out like arc light, this is something more. As you know, I didn't invade your mental privacy but I did take the liberty of seeking a few answers. Those answers may shake you.'

He turned quickly. 'Come on up to the hotel.'

'I want answers on the way,' said Travers.

'You mean you don't know? God, I'd heard that love blinds you but this is ridiculous.'

Travers grinned. Under normal circumstances the words might have caused offence but he could feel both affection and genuine pleasure clothing the words.

'Spell it out,' he said.

'Its simple enough, you're one.'

'Eh?'

'Open up, please.'

'Fine, fine. Now this is the point, I can't contact just you, Bill, I can only contact you both. Telepathically you're one, you're linked. Together, you make *one complete being* and make me realize I'm only half a human. I shall never be unless I meet and link up with my reciprocal opposite. This must be part of the new order under the new laws which apply now.'

He paused and frowned. 'There's one thing you ought to know. It isn't pretty but I have to tell you. You can never live alone again, if one dies, the other follows immediately. It's as decisive and as final as the head being severed from the body.'

They reached out and found each other's hands.

'That part we already knew,' said Lisa softly.

## CHAPTER SIX

They emerged from the trees and crossed a wide, slightly over-grown lawn. Beyond, the grey stone of the hotel rose in front of them. It was a small but well constructed building, skilfully contrived to blend with its surroundings. Behind it was a long, clear mountain lake.

Travers, noting points, decided that it must have been prohibitively expensive a week ago—. A week? Only a week? Yes, it was. Funny that, just a week ago he was making his last call, trying to sell to that prickly bastard Krane. Yet only a few hours later—

'All systems function,' said Robinson as they entered the building. 'The place has its own generating system and there is enough in the deep freeze for several weeks although our numbers are increasing daily.'

He smiled at Lisa. 'Good news for you. A lady who booked here and never arrived sent on a pile of new dresses in advance. At a guess, I'd say she was around your size. However, I'm sure you both want a bath, a meal and time to relax. Oh, one thing, mental privacy is a strict rule here but we'd like you to be open for anything urgent.'

He paused by the elevator. 'Room nineteen has been set

aside for you. If it's all right with you, we'd like to hold a sort of get-together around seven—.'

In one of the smaller lounges, three men were seated in the comfortable chairs.

Robinson waved a casual introduction. 'From left to right, Herr Pabst, Mr Salter and Mr Nasuki.'

Travers looked them over quickly. Pabst was a large, jovial-looking man with greying hair. Salter was tall, thin and solemn. Nasuki was bright eyed, smiling and delicately boned.

'If you will be good enough to open your minds just a little more.'

They complied and both became aware of a bond between them all. Their thinking, principles, standards and attitudes to life had a common foundation.

Travers found himself grinning rather idiotically. He liked these people.

There was no doubt that the feeling was mutual.

'Old blubber lips chose well,' said Pabst with a smile.

Robinson only laughed and Travers nodded to himself understandingly. Under normal circumstances, the remark could well have caused offence but now, names by themselves meant nothing. It was the *feeling* which came with the words which counted and the words had come with genuine respect and friendship.

Pabst drew up chairs for them. 'Please sit down. The object of this conference is an exchange of information. However, as new arrivals, we feel it only right and proper for you to start the ball rolling. I take it you have many questions to ask?'

Travers grinned. 'Too many but I'll try and sort them

out in order of importance. First—' he opened his mind more—'this is all I know and the conclusions I have drawn.'

Pabst nodded. 'Almost in agreement with our own conclusions. We also decided that the entire race had contracted what might be termed a parapsychic infection. The race is telepathic, can transport objects not only from one place to another but can bring them into being from elsewhere. The individual can transport himself from one place to another and can kill by a minor effort of will. He can cause fires and extinguish them by the same method. He can impose illusions on other minds often fatal illusions. Over limited areas he can command the weather and, we must assume, put into practice all the other known phenomena on the subject.'

He paused and smiled sadly. 'Only one facet of this vast field seems to have escaped us and that is precognition. I must confess I am not sorry about that, it could well have been the last straw.'

He paused again and looked at them both sombrely. 'One vital factor you have missed—as a race *we are pillaging the universe*.'

Travers went cold inside. Beamish's death ray! He had thought about it at the time but had never followed it up in his thoughts to a logical conclusion.

The Master, too, had been filching weapons, technologies and God knew what else for all he was worth. How many others were doing the same?

'How long before certain races take exception to being robbed?' enquired Lisa, taking up the continuation of his thoughts.

Pabst nodded quickly. 'That worries us a hell of a lot also. You see, the faculty doesn't stop at material objects. Facts and information are there for the taking, tell them about Prokof, Robinson.'

The negro leaned forward in his chair. 'He was a personal friend, one of us but, perhaps over eager. He asked for a solution to our present problem, it was an act from which we must all take warning. We believe he got the answer but the capacity of the human brain is limited. It was, we think, a case of too much information and it blew his mind like a fuse.'

Pabst said quietly: 'Consider the common ground which unites us. Principles, integrity, the ideal of forming a stable society and think of the opposite side of the coin. Others have learned command words, the gang boss, the potential dictator and, perhaps the most dangerous of all, the outwardly respectable.'

'And sooner or later it's going to come to a show-down,' suggested Travers.

'As I see it, it's unavoidable.'

'Aside from known benevolent aliens, what about the others? I've seen others.'

'We also. Unfortunately we do not know what channels our powers have opened. Your own experience is a pointer, how did your green cat get to earth. I suspect some dear old lady who wanted a cat. One loose, careless command and there you are. No type of cat was specified, just a vague picture.'

Travers leaned forward. 'That brings me to the most important and most frightening question of all.'

'Yes?' Pabst was intent.

'Right, when I give a command, to *whom*, or to *what* do I give the command?'

'The answer to that is brief and pointed—*yourself*.'

'Pardon!'

'Sorry,' Pabst smiled. 'Too brief and too pointed. We think it goes something like this, Bill. Permeating the universe is a *force*, a power, something which is *there*. A wholly impersonal power, cosmic energy or solar radiation could be used as excellent parallels although I don't think it is either. Whatever it was that hit us, stimulated, or brought into being, some section of the brain which can utilize this power. When you give a command, you merely issue instructions to yourself as to how that power should be applied. Put another way, you punch out a programme and the power complies with your instructions.'

'Why an impersonal power?'

'It doesn't differentiate, does it? It carries out your commands irrespective of results. It cannot interpret, if the commands are vague, the results are vague. As you have seen, commands are carried out regardless of whether the results are fatal.'

Pabst paused and lit a long cigar. 'Take my own experiences. I am—was—a biophysicist, the creative and preventive medicine angle. I was staying in an hotel in Hamburg when I thought I heard a muffled scream in the next room.

'I went to investigate and found the door bulging outwards. It came open easily when I pulled the handle and I was almost swept off my feet by a flood of money. There were American dollars, British pounds, marks, liras and every coin under the sun. It was clear, later, what had happened. My room neighbour had discovered his powers and wished himself a billion or something equally ridiculous. He got it and it killed him. It filled the room and he died of suffocation.

'When I checked round the hotel, there was only one man in it. He was wandering round the lounge and asked me where he was. Apparently his wife had told him to get lost and it was impossible to explain to him. He refused to believe it—*couldn't* believe it.'

'You are joking. This is Seattle. I work in the bank here. How can this possibly be an hotel in Hamburg, Germany?'

Robinson took over. 'I was a psychiatrist, attending a conference in Geneva. There were some Southerners, tourists presumably, staying at the same hotel. Although they said nothing, their expressions indicated that they found my presence distasteful.

'On waking the following morning, in a weak moment, I wished myself white. On looking in the mirror, I had the shock of my life. I was white but most definitely not Caucasian. I was alabaster, I was a whited sepulchre.'

Salter said: 'I have always been a compulsive traveller and I was foolish enough to wish I was in Sicily. Friends, I made it fine. I found myself on the top of Mount Etna, tottering on the edge of the crater.'

Nasuki, the tiny Japanese smiled at Lisa. 'I am the only one present without regret for a first command—how old would you say I am, young lady?'

Lisa smiled back. 'I flatter myself I'm rather good at this—thirty.'

'Correct yet not correct. I am ninety-two years of age.'

His smile seemed to come from within and set them all smiling.

'I was bed-ridden and dying. I had been bed-ridden for nine years. When I awoke on that morning, there was no nurse. There was no one to give the drugs and injections which kept my weary old heart beating. I was vaguely alarmed but not unduly so and I wished briefly that I was thirty years old again.'

He paused and was suddenly serious. 'We must never forget that we are survivors. We temper the terrors of past experience with humour but let us remember the lost. The thousands who just wished themselves elsewhere and whose frozen bodies may now be drifting in space. Yet others who are lost and find themselves on alien worlds so far away that their distance defies the imagination.'

He stopped and smiled apologetically. 'I am sorry to sound depressing but when I look back, when we all look back, we could have ended up the same way.'

Pabst's prediction that opposition might come from the outwardly respectable proved wholly true.

His name was Willis Quade and, beside him, the criminal elements rapidly faded into insignificance.

He was—had been—a mathematician employed by a minor university on the outskirts of a large industrial city.

Quade was forty-five years old, pink faced, balding and inclined to stoutness. To his few friends and immediate colleagues, he was a quiet, rather reserved man of moderate habits. Inwardly, he was an imprisoned but calculating monster. He had, of course, his moments, usually in the red light districts of remote cities where he was unknown.

In his immediate surroundings, however, his conduct was above reproach. Quade was as he was because he was restrained by the possible consequences of doing otherwise. Arrest, or the condemnation of public opinion, would deprive him of his livelihood and all its attendant advantages. Inside him, however, something which would have shocked his colleagues, paced restlessly up and down in a torment of frustration.

When he awoke on that particular morning, a minor whim for a lighted cigarette brought immediate response.

He looked at the smoking white cylinder between his fingers, startled but unfrightened.

Then he said: 'Go out!'

It was immediately extinguished.

Quade's mathematical mind began to put two and two together. For an hour or two he experimented, moving objects about the room and generally testing his powers. He saw the need of a command word and within a short time felt he had a grip on the situation.

His next move was to discover if the phenomena applied only to himself or to others. A brief glance out of the window assured him that it was world-wide.

The street below was a chaos of stalled traffic and panic-stricken people.

He saw men and women vanish, re-appear, only to vanish again. A few dedicated policemen were struggling desperately but hopelessly to restore some sort of order.

He saw an empty vehicle nearly run a policeman down. The man flung himself out of the way, turned and, a second later, the vehicle exploded.

Quade thought about that. What had caused the vehicle

to explode? After some considered thought, he decided he had the answer—the angry and frightened policeman was responsible.

It was easy enough to check on. He leaned out of the window, selected a green vehicle on the opposite side of the road and said: 'Blast you!'

The green car immediately blew up in a cloud of flame and black smoke.

Quade withdrew from the window, smiling to himself. He had been right, the policeman had probably used exactly the same words only those words had force now.

He sat down on the edge of his unmade bed, one thought filling his mind—*he was free.*

He was not, however, a fool. His next move was to *think* how best to use the present situation to his own advantage. He was sharply aware that the economy of the entire world had collapsed. A note of any denomination of any country in the world was now of less value than a sheet of toilet paper. Jewels, precious stones and metals were valueless because they could not relate to money. Works of art, mere whims to surviving art lovers.

There was but one remaining commodity and that was *power*. Most certainly it was available to all, but very few, apparently, had begun to control it.

The next step, therefore, was to ascertain its limitations, if any, and apply it. He had no doubt that others had drawn similar conclusions but here initiative really counted. One must become an adept, a master, so skilled in application that no possible opposition could stand against him. His diversions, therefore, must wait.

Quade saw clearly that civilization had come to an end,

it was the death of a technological culture. Within two months, famine and disease would start taking their toll.

Quade tried out some experiments in his front room and finally took the plunge on teleportation. The command that he arrive safely at his brother's house deposited him safely on the front lawn. It was a big rambling building on the outskirts of a small town.

He had no doubt that the building was empty. His brother had always been highly strung and inclined to panic.

He was correct. The house was empty and a half-eaten meal lay on the table.

Quade looked the place over. There were ample stocks of canned food but the contents of the deep freeze were, he decided, suspect.

No point in hanging around, he had already decided on a plan. First he used his powers to cleanse the immediate sewers and dispose of bad food.

There was a large swimming pool at the back, he purified that for his immediate drinking purposes.

Next he turned his attention to the town. 'I command that all corpses in this town are immediately incinerated together with rotting food and similar decaying matter.'

Brief puffs of black smoke rose from various parts of the town.

When everything was cleaned to his satisfaction, he turned his attention to the second part of his plan. He began to sweep the area telepathically for survivors and the first he found was Dace.

Sheer terror accounted for Dace's survival, a terror

now bordering on the catatonic. He was a big, hairy man who had once worked on a local construction site.

He was a slow thinking, not too intelligent man and a series of bewildering and terrifying teleportations had almost deprived him of the will to think.

An idle desire to see his sister had transported him to New York State where, shocked beyond measure, he had immediately wished himself back. A casual thought whisked him to Africa, another to the Arctic from whence he had once again returned with a frost-bitten finger. After which his mind had dried up.

Quade took him over telepathically and enslaved him completely. If Quade had ordered him to cut his own throat slowly with a jagged knife, Dace would have done so.

In two days, Quade controlled the lives of forty-three men and twenty-five women. He was basically a sadistic man but his faculties had given him insight into human psychology. He saw to it that his slaves *enjoyed* their servitude. He imposed feelings of gratitude for their 'rescue' and dependence on him alone for their future safety and peace of mind. By the time he had finished with them, he had not only their abject obedience but something very close to worship

Quade smiled to himself. The only commodity was power and he was accumulating that faster than anyone had ever accumulated wealth.

He began to comb the country for experts in various fields particularly those in military spheres. He was no soldier but he could always drain the information from others.

At the same time he was cautiously availing himself of superior knowledge. He had seen, as Travers had seen, that there were limits and dangers inherent in the acquisition of alien weapons. He had never heard of Prokof but his logical mind told him that there were limits to the capacity of the human brain to absorb knowledge.

In this sphere, therefore, all his seeking was prefixed by, 'within the scope of my normal intelligence.'

Despite his caution, he managed to obtain some hideous instruments of destruction although several had to be hastily disposed of. His slaves were put to the unenviable task of testing them out, well clear of the town.

Within a month, he had a thousand men under his command plus a certain smug satisfaction. With these thousand men, plus their weapons, he could have conquered the past world of pre-epidemic days.

There were, however, side-effects of which he was unaware and had never considered.

As Travers had reasoned with Beamish's death-ray, it had come from somewhere. Quade's weapons had come from somewhere and weapons which came from somewhere *brought other things with them.*

They brought life in the form of micro-organisms, minute spores and seeds. There was a law within the new law which was now applicable to Earth—such life tended to be attracted to motivation. As Quade's motivation was primarily the acquisition of power, the lifeforms tended to be hostile. He was not to find out about this until much later.

He also had a lot to learn. So intent had he been on

consolidating his position that he had had little time to check the opposition.

He did not know there were aliens on the planet or that others, diametrically opposed to all he stood for, were growing in strength in the mountains.

He realized there must be opposition but his first actual contact with any sort of organized force was a chance detection of a megalomaniac calling himself 'The Master'.

In the last few months, the Master had built himself an army of considerable size but limited discipline.

The first Quade knew of his existence was a whispering sound high in the air but he made no attempt to see the high flying aircraft. Instead he read the pilot telepathically and, by so doing, opened the way for a complete survey.

The aircraft itself was one of ten, constructed by alien methods and propelled by an entirely revolutionary power system. Its armament, too, was devastating but—yet to be discovered—became unstable in prolonged operation. It had not been designed for this world and became unstable in the lesser gravity of Earth.

Through this contact also Quade learned that there were aliens in the vicinity. He was not unduly concerned as yet, let the Master have a go first, he might succeed. If he didn't, he, Quade, could watch and profit by his mistakes. He selected a small number of the Master's field staff as observers, through their eyes he could telepathically watch the battle.

He looked at the set-up critically. A fair amount of armour had been accumulated, mostly obsolete but sufficient for an armoured thrust.

Generally speaking, the rabble of infantry was armed

with conventional weapons although a percentage carried black rods terminating in a white bulb. These weapons undoubtedly had an alien origin.

The troops and transports were packed together tightly, an open invitation to any skilled gun crew to chop them to pieces.

Quade appreciated that the Master was depending on his mental canopy but a few casual probes had revealed a glaring weakness. Presumably the Master was labouring under the delusion that he held a monopoly on parapsychic manipulation. The canopy was capable of resisting almost anything save parapsychic attack.

Quade made a brief survey of the Master's army and permitted himself a faint smile. Morale sagged badly in all sectors and discipline was superficial. Most of the men were there because they felt secure among others. It gave them something to do and it helped having someone tell them what to do.

Quade decided that if the opening of the attack was successful it would probably be followed through. Stiff opposition, however, would reduce the troops to panic within seconds. Morale would collapse and there would be chaos.

The Master had set the time of attack for noon and, at three minutes to the hour, the aircraft came in. They were flying too high to be seen but the sound of their passing was clearly audible.

The troops looked up hopefully. They had been told that the planes would go in first to soften up the defences.

Seconds later there was a whistling noise and something black crashed among the trees about a mile distant.

High up a single parachute blossomed and part of an aircraft wing came fluttering down like a silver leaf.

There had been no flash and no explosion but it was clear that the softening up process had never got going.

A whistle blew and Quade noticed that there were other alien weapons besides those he had already noticed.

These resembled rather fat telescopes on tripods and were positioned slightly in front of the waiting troops.

As the whistle blew, the operators pulled a fat red lever set at the rear end of the telescopes.

The weapons made a screaming noise and ejected a rapid series of glowing blue spheres not unlike normal tracer save that they were as big as tennis balls.

The spheres vanished into a line of trees some four hundred yards distant, turning four into brief vapour en route.

It appeared to Quade that somewhere among the trees they struck something invisible for they appeared to ricochet. Many came back in what seemed a leisurely but oddly erratic way.

The first took an ancient howitzer and entire crew and puffed them out of existence. The second hit a light tank and transformed it into a thick cloud of grey smoke. The third collided with another sphere going out and the resultant detonation wiped out the first line of armour—about thirty tanks.

As Quade had anticipated, morale cracked completely. Ricocheting blue spheres on their erratic trajectories were now coming back at all angles.

Advancing armour turned away, colliding with other vehicles turning in the opposite direction.

Soldiers were throwing away their arms and running only to be cut down by more experienced troops in a vain effort to restore order.

In many places men and, very often whole groups of men, simply vanished.

Quade turned his attention to the object of the attack and for the first time felt a twinge of alarm.

A mental probe of the barrier produced a tingling impact in his mind very much like an electric shock. It left him with a numb feeling inside his head which lasted for several hours.

He did, however, learn two facts from the experience. First, the barrier was sentient and, second, it was the antithesis of all he stood for.

The barrier was impenetrable both to physical force and parapsychic attack. It possessed the unique quality, in all spheres of reversing the forces exerted against it and thus hurling them back. The greater the degree of force, the greater the capacity of the barrier to hurl it back. It was like throwing highly inflammable fuel on an already raging fire.

The only way to penetrate the barrier was a complete and permanent character change. Under the new laws such a thing was possible but Quade knew this was out. He didn't *want* to change his character and, even if he did, what was the point? Once changed, his reasons for wishing to do so would no longer be valid.

## CHAPTER SEVEN

Quade decided that he could afford to wait. In the meantime, there were about twelve thousand survivors of the battle to be coerced into his service. Before that, however, there was a little experiment he wanted to try out—.

The Master had survived the battle but defeat had done nothing for his mental stability. He sat on the wreck of a burned-out truck biting his nails and trying to determine who was responsible for his downfall.

In the middle of his contemplation, a small red flame appeared on the third knuckle of his left hand.

The Master stared at it, then brought the palm of his right hand down on the flame.

When he removed it, however, the flame was not only still there but had transferred a similar flame to his right thumb.

The Master stared desperately about him and saw, not twenty feet distant, a small stream. He ran to it and thrust his hands into the deepest part of the icy water he could find.

He was horrified to see the flames still burning beneath

the surface. He thrust them deeper into the sand and mud at the bottom of the stream.

When he withdrew them, the flames still burned steadily and the little finger of his left hand was also alight.

The pain was agonizing, his fingers felt as if they were being pressed to a red hot stove.

Abruptly the fingers of both hands ignited and the flames leapt higher. The pain became unbearable and his mind cracked.

He ran across the deserted battlefield, leaping over bodies and dodging round wrecked vehicles, screaming.

As he ran, he beat at his body and, where his hands touched, the flames took hold.

Soon he was a running effigy, no longer human, red flames streaming out behind him.

He began to slow, lurching from side to side and then, suddenly, the flames engulfed him. Briefly, the shimmering outline of a human form seemed to hang in the air and then all was gone. Only a few white flakes of ash drifting down to the grass showed that he had ever existed.

Quade smiled to himself, it had been an informative diversion but he regretted that the Master had been too deranged to fight back.

In the mountains, numbers had increased dramatically but fortunately many experts in various fields were included. Experts who turned their skills and faculties to food production and building. Small, single storey living units now completely encircled the lake.

The settlement now consisted of forty-three thousand

men and thirty-two thousand women, all of whom had been selected. It was estimated that at least four million would eventually be drawn in.

The weekly conference concentrated on the immediate danger.

'We should be impregnable,' said Salter.

'The words "should be" are not enough,' said Robinson.

'I agree.' Pabst looked worried. 'Quade has one supreme advantage over us all and that is utter ruthlessness. We are restrained by our natures, by the basic principles which unite us. He is restrained by nothing.'

Travers said: 'We have been discussing this subject. We have one advantage. One move which Quade is psychologically incapable of making.'

They looked at him or, more aptly, they looked at them both. To outsiders Travers and Lisa spoke as one.

'What advantage, what move?' asked Robinson.

'We could call someone in to help us.'

'An alien, you mean?' He frowned. 'Is that wise?'

'Is it wise not to do so? We need representation, we need expert advice. If we don't call someone in soon, how much longer before someone in the universe calls us out? Quade is not the only one taking what he wants.'

'Aliens are caring for the children,' Nasuki reminded them quietly. 'I think we have a point worth considering.'

'Why can't Quade do the same?' asked Robinson.

'And admit to himself that he needs help? Consider the dangers for him. That same someone might take over and dispose of his host.'

Pabst laughed. 'Quade will think of that first. I must

agree, he's psychologically incapable of making such a move. Yes, I must agree with this suggestion but first, in view of its importance, it must be submitted to the entire settlement. If we get an affirmative and I think we will, we all co-operate on a special command.'

None of them knew quite what to expect but the result was immediate. There was a faint wind-sound and then a man stood among them.

The man wore a long red cloak which reached almost to his heels. His hands were white and beautifully shaped. He had a mane of silver-grey hair but the face—somehow the face escaped them. Somehow it always seemed turned away or lost in shadow. It was an implied face and no one could distinguish its features.

'The name is Akron,' said the man in what seemed a perfectly normal voice. 'My telepathic faculty is such that it effects that part of the mind which interprets sound. You think you are hearing me but you are not. You, Herr Pabst, speak fluent English because you have travelled extensively both in the United States and in England but you are hearing me in German, are you not?'

'God, yes, but I hadn't realized it until you drew my attention to it.'

'Our Japanese friends and all other nationals present are likewise hearing me in their own languages. I must stress, however, that I shall respect your mental privacy unless requested otherwise.'

'We'll open up,' said Robinson quickly.

'Thank you.' Somehow Akron conveyed the impression of a faint smile. 'I puzzle you. My near-normal appearance is a gesture of courtesy. I do not look like you and, to be specific, I do not look like anything you have ever imagined or ever can imagine.'

He paused and appeared to smile at them. 'Thank you for your invitation but, before turning to immediate problems, I would like to make my position clear. I am not here at immense sacrifice nor am I a do-gooder. I am here because I wish to be, because my nature is such that I am stimulated by the problems which confront you. Their prosecution and final solution will be its own reward. I therefore require no remuneration of any kind. My services place you under no obligation whatever, real or implied. You, Mr Travers, will fully understand this, as you have already had dealings with mature outworlders.'

Travers nodded. Here again was no false sentiment. It was another case of alien intelligence doing a job because he liked doing that kind of job.

Akron continued. 'I knew of your problems. I have given them much thought before my arrival but I could do nothing until you sent for me.'

He paused and appeared to look at them all. 'I perceive that some of you find this strange. Pause to consider, please. A doctor may perceive certain signs of illness as he passes you in the street but he can do nothing until you send for him. Similarly, a lawyer may be aware of countless legal problems confronting you but he cannot help until you consult him professionally. This fact applies here—I had to be called.'

The head seemed to turn towards someone at the back of the room. 'No, Mr Roach, I am not here as a military adviser. The man, Quade, is the least of your worries. We may, perhaps, concern ourselves with him when immediate problems have been dealt with.'

It seemed to Travers that the red cloak changed briefly to a beautiful blue but he was never sure.

The alien continued. 'I must tell you that this present gathering has imposed certain restraints on the mature intelligences abounding in the universe. Restraints and no little consternation. All are amazed at the speed with which your culture has formed a small but wholly stable nucleus in the midst of chaos. But for this, measures would have been taken against you. As it stands now, however, they are prepared to wait and observe. They are even prepared to endure, tolerantly, the wholesale plundering of the disbalanced members of your culture.'

He appeared to grow slightly in stature. 'You have, therefore, bought yourself breathing space but, on the other hand, no human being can escape the consequences of this plundering. Many of you have reported the presence of aliens. I must inform you that your world now abounds with aliens. Alien lifeforms, alien micro-organisms and alien plants.

'Again I must refer to Mr Travers who encountered an alien cat, one of fifty-six thousand other lifeforms now surviving on Earth. He also met a youth with an alien weapon. Fourteen thousand, eight hundred and six weapons have been brought to Earth in this way. This does not include the countless new technologies purloined for similar ends.'

The alien made a brief sweeping gesture. 'The world you knew is passing forever, all of you must come to terms with the new one. With due respect, you are developing a garrison mentality, you are not a beleagured settlement yet.'

He appeared to look directly at Travers and Lisa. 'You would do well to retrace your steps across country to the inn. Yes, I see you glancing at the window. I am well aware that it is winter, that there are several feet of snow and possibly worse weather to come. However, I must remind you all, that you are perfectly capable of adjusting to extremes of temperature. Note, please, that herein is an important lesson. It is for you to adapt to conditions and *not* the reverse. As you all know, it is possible to command warm weather to a limited area but consider the repercussions. Plants might blossom, birds might mate but, when you move on, you could leave death behind you. Do not part the waters of a swift river—perhaps causing major floods upstream—when you are perfectly capable of walking on its surface. There are countless other examples but these two will suffice. Now, my friends, go out in your world and learn to live with it. In the meantime, remember, you are still telepathically in contact. The weekly conferences, therefore, may continue as usual—.'

Travers found it was easy enough to give the command but difficult to believe in it. The snow *looked* cold, icicles hung from branches and the wind howled mournfully.

He shifted his rucksack to a more comfortable position and smiled at Lisa. 'We would have to be the first.'

Pabst patted his shoulder. 'Good luck—you've used snow shoes before?—fine.'

The wind howled louder when they opened the door and they were both shocked to find it only mild but blustery. Both were well aware that the thermometer registered fifteen below.

He bent down, grasped a handful of snow and shook his head. 'Tepid snow, now I've seen everything.'

He dropped the snow and took her hand. 'I love you.'

'I know, but I shall never get tired of hearing it.'

'Under normal circumstances I should never have allowed you to come. Some of this journey may be very dangerous.'

She squeezed his hand. 'A lot of it is going to be heaven.'

On the third day out, they received a telepathic message from Akron.

'One mile, directly ahead of you, you will find a granite rock shoulder rising to the height of fifty feet. Move to the eastern side of this rock. You will find a fissure about five feet wide and eight feet deep. Make all possible speed to the rock, enter the fissure and stay there.'

'What the devil was that all about?' Travers looked worried. 'Let's get moving.'

They reached the rock shoulder and flung themselves down in the fissure, slightly breathless.

'I have a feeling of urgency,' she said.

They waited, hand in hand, conscious of a rising tension.

'Foreboding,' he corrected. 'And I don't care for it.'

He glanced upwards. 'More snow on the way, I think—.'

He never finished the sentence. The clouds lit as if an enormous light had been switched on behind them. It was a peculiarly unnatural light, eye-searing, yellowish yet tinged with scarlet.

Before either of them could comment, the earth punched upwards at their bodies. The force of the impact lifted them in the air and deposited them outside the fissure.

Instinctively he had held on to her hand and tried to drag her back to safety as soon as he realized what had happened.

Before he could do so, a fissure opened in the earth some hundred feet away. Six trees toppled sideways with a rending sound and a snapping of branches.

Somehow the incident galvanized him to unnatural efforts. He dragged her back to safety and flung himself on the top of her. He knew he had to protect her from what he sensed was coming although he had no idea what it was.

The sky darkened suddenly and the first manifestation was sound. It came with a howling shriek which deafened them both and he realized what it was—wind. But no wind or tornado in all Earth's history had ever blown with such stupefying force.

Daylight vanished completely as the wind swept its burden above them.

He had a confused impression of soil, boulders and branches hurtling past. He saw hundred foot trees careening above, roots intact, plucked from the soil by the force of the wind.

It was, he discovered, only the beginning. What followed was close to a volcanic eruption. The fissure lit redly to a hurricane of swirling red sparks. Among the sparks were blazing tree trunks, trailing flame, white hot boulders and streaming smoke.

Travers was numbed but he figured that the hurricane of fire lasted at least three minutes before it began to ease. It was then he was glad of the fissure for, as the wind lessened, things fell from the sky. A rain of hot soil, blazing branches, smoking tree trunks and glowing boulders.

Finally—it seemed hours later—the wind faded and things stopped dropping from the sky.

They sat shakily upright and stared in front of them. Neither spoke, both of them realized the impossibility of comment.

In front of the fissure had been a forest of tall densely packed trees. Between them snow had been three feet deep and, where drifts had formed, twelve feet deep. The snow had vanished and, as far as they could see, most of the trees had been snapped off close to the ground. Here and there, solitary and blackened trunks still stood but completely stripped of branches. Numerous fires still burned and they could feel the heat on their faces.

The whole scene reminded Travers of the war. He had seen a woodland like this once—after several hours of concentrated shelling.

He put his arm round her. 'You all right, my dearest?'

'A bit numb, darling, but unhurt. What about you? You lay on top of me to protect me.'

'I liked that part,' he said with a lightness he was far from feeling.

She was not deceived. 'We're both pretty badly shaken up, my love. What do you think it was?'

'I can only guess.' He shook his head worriedly. 'I'd say it was some kind of explosion but if it was it made a hydro-nuclear device look like a damp match.'

'When it cools down a little, shall we climb to the top of the cliff?'

They were compelled to wait two hours but when they reached the summit neither of them could find words.

After some seconds she said: 'Where is the mountain, our mountain?'

'Where is the entire range of which it was a part? The whole damn lot has gone. Say, our friends! We'd better check.'

He gradually relaxed. 'Everyone we know responded and could confirm the survival of many others.'

He frowned thoughtfully. 'Lisa, Akron knew this was going to happen. He got us away not only to adjust to new conditions but to ensure our survival.'

She looked up into his face. 'Quade?'

'I don't know. It seemed a little too big for Quade.'

'Then who?'

'I don't know.' He became worried again. 'The children! They're only seventy miles from here. I'd better check.'

As the alien had told him, telepathic recognition was immediate.

'The children are safe, Mr Travers, but I knew you would make sure. You will recall, we are in a deep valley and fortunately the barrier was well able to resist the fading blast. I am looking forward to meeting you again as obviously you will come this way.'

'Yes, we shall and thank you.'

He broke contact and looked at Lisa. 'You got all that?'

'Of course. When you receive, I receive.'

He took her hand in his. 'Let's get moving and get clear of this wilderness.'

It was several hours before signs of devastation began to

fade and whole trees began to replace the shattered ones. Patches of snow began to appear but it was late afternoon before things looked nearly normal again.

'Stop here?'

'Fine, I'll fix you a meal.'

The food was different to their first meal in the wilds. A Japanese nutritions expert had teamed up with an American agronomist and between them they had created a new vegetable. It looked like a huge carrot but it contained a wholly balanced diet. It tasted rather like an earthy sort of apple but was very satisfying.

Just as they finished, there was a brief air disturbance and Akron appeared.

His appearance startled Travers and he said, awkwardly. 'We're honoured, a personal visit.'

'Certainly a personal visit. Is it not reasonable that I should confer first with the only *whole* member of your race?'

'I don't follow you.'

'The others are, as yet, incomplete. Your race only becomes whole when reciprocal male unites with reciprocal female, making one *complete* human being.'

'But it was sheer chance, we—.'

'I am well aware of what took place. The factor you fail to realize is, that neither of you would have considered such a telepathic revelation unless you wholly complemented one another.

'However, to continue. Since my arrival, many things have come to my attention. One, already mentioned, is the speed with which—no disrespect—a minus culture could so rapidly form a stable nucleus. Before the sudden inception of your faculties, you were compelled to steady your tottering society by force. You needed punitive laws and a veritable army of police to hold it erect. Not, one notes, with startling success. Periodically, it could not be maintained beyond a national scale and war broke out.

'From another angle, technical progress was so far in advance of cultural growth that any viewing sociologist would have been deeply disturbed. In short, you were a mess and the present situation gives rise to many pointed questions.'

Travers said: 'So?' in a puzzled voice.

'I am not the one asking the pointed questions. The most pointed question of all, which most of the intelligences in the Universe are asking is—who knew the answers?'

'I'm afraid I'm not with you.'

'Someone knew all the answers, Mr Travers, and that someone just tried to remove you and all your friends.'

'Quade?'

'Hardly. The eruption undermined his confidence badly and he is still alarmed.'

'Then who?'

'That is the pointed question. I can think of only twenty races in the Universe capable of transmitting anti-matter impulses over light-distances to assemble themselves correctly in the core of a mountain.'

'Parapsychic means?'

Akron shook his head. 'Many many races, my own included, can detect such manipulation. Such methods would leave imprints which would remain for several days.'

Travers thought about it. 'The question which occurs to me is, why?'

'You anticipate me. When we have the answer to that question, we shall have an answer to all.'

'You have no idea yourself?'

'I have the ideas, Mr Travers, but I need time to test and confirm them. With your permission, I shall have to call in other intelligences to further my research, I shall have a theory which I believe to be correct and, by the time you reach the inn, I should have confirmed it. I will meet you there.'

'Well, thank you for all you have done and are doing.'

'Do not be too pleased. Confirmation of my theory, will only tell us why. It will not tell us *who* and discovering who might well prove fatal for us all. I shall see you at the inn.'

Without warning, he vanished.

They were silent for a long while, then Travers said: 'I shall want at least two days to think things over.'

'We shall,' she agreed.

'It's been the hell of a day, hasn't it?'

She put her arms round his neck. 'Day is over, night is beginning. Shall we provide a contrast?'

It was Lisa who awoke in the early hours of the morning and squeezed Travers' naked shoulder.

He moved from sleep to wakefulness instantly.

'What is it, darling?'

'Someone is probing telepathically. I probably got it first because she's a woman.'

Travers knew it was a stranger, they were open telepathically to anyone they knew.

'Does it feel safe?'

'I can't tell, very cautious like someone knocking on a door a long way away.'

'We can't afford to take chances, might be a sort of female Quade.'

'We could command information,' she suggested.

'An excellent idea.'

A few seconds later they looked at each other. The woman was not hostile but she was wise and carefully shielded.

'We'll open up a little,' he suggested. 'Make it neat and terse like a radio transmitter—receiving you.'

'I can't read you.'

'You're not intended to. We're playing it safe like you.'

'I hope to stay safe but I have an idea. I have just passed through a sort of children's refuge. If you're genuine, you could check with one of the aliens.'

Travers laughed softly. 'No need, if you came through the settlement you're one of us—opening up.'

There was a brief pause then: 'You feel nice, thank God I've made contact at last but what makes you so strong?'

'There are two of us.'

'A second, please. Yes, yes, I perceive it now but you come over as one.' Then: 'Ah I have it now, I can feel it, you're in love. No wonder you felt nice.'

'Where are you? Never mind, I get the picture. We should be with you in about an hour.'

It was dawn when they reached her and the first thing

they noticed was her smile. It lit the small brown face almost to light.

She held out both her hands. 'Bill, Lisa, thank heaven to meet someone who feels the same, lives the same.'

'You're Indian.'

'Pakistan. My name is Ursula Surbanah. My father wanted me to have an English first name. I went to England to look after him but I had only been there a week when—.'

She left the sentence unfinished and sat down on a fallen branch.

She was tiny and slender and moved with a grace which was almost artistic.

'You're wise,' said Lisa thoughtfully. 'You're shielded, you've obviously learned how to adapt to extremes of temperature and you got here from England somehow.'

'True but the learning was hard. One has to learn when one is alone. Someone wished my father dead, you see—.' Again she left the sentence unfinished.

'You seem to have learned very well.'

'Yes, due to a dreadful but fortunate mistake, I placed myself in a position where I had to think. When all this terror began, like many, I panicked. You see, *I wished myself back a day.*'

## CHAPTER EIGHT

She paused and looked up at them. 'I have often wondered if there were others who made the same mistake, it was a dreadful experience. It was like being two people. I crouched there in my own mind watching myself do all the things I had done the day before. I said the same things, thought the same things but there was nothing I could do to change anything. I watched myself think "I must make the bed now" and "did I turn off that kettle?" things like that.

'I knew I was going to drop and break the blue plate but I could do nothing about it. I knew I was going to burn my hand in the oven. I did and it hurt for a long time just the same.

'The worst part was when my father came home for dinner and I could do nothing to warn him. I said the same futile ordinary things I had said the day before.

'I wanted to tell him that in a few hours everything would be madness, that he must not go out the following morning but I was just trapped within myself.'

She paused briefly, then continued. 'However, it did give me time to think. I thought if someone could wish my father dead—"drop dead, you bloody wog"—were the exact words, then someone could wish me dead. So I wished—ordered—that they couldn't. Then I saw how vulnerable I was to a casual wish and thought out a command word.'

Lisa patted her shoulder. 'And you've been alone since then?'

'I was frightened. So many dead and so many, many horrible men. I wanted to get away from London, somewhere different, somewhere there was a lot of open space and clean air. So I came—teleported myself to Canada and, several months later, I found the children and the aliens.'

'The barrier let you through?'

'I didn't know there was a barrier until the aliens told me. I stayed under their protection until they told me someone like myself was coming. So I set out to meet you and kept calling.'

'Do you think you actually re-lived a complete day?' asked Travers.

'I don't know. It could have happened in my mind. I have learned that not everything is *real* if you understand me. Some of it is—I can't think of the word.'

'Subjective?' he suggested.

'Yes, that's it, subjective. I met a horrible man who tried to enslave me. He said if I didn't take all my clothes off, he would call up the devil to chastise me.'

A smile touched the corners of her mouth. 'I wouldn't, so he carried out his threat. The earth split open and flames gushed out. Then this goat-thing with little horns and a hooked nose appeared. I remember thinking "I've seen pictures of the devil exactly like this."

'There was a lot of thunder and lightning and this

thing stamped around me with sparks shooting from its cloven hoofs. It didn't frighten me because I couldn't believe in it. I knew it came from the man's mind although I realize it could have hurt me but for my command.'

Travers looked at her with respect. 'Ursula, you're no damn fool.' A thought occurred to him. 'You had been in England a week?'

'Yes.'

'How much English do you speak?'

She looked puzzled. 'A little, very badly.'

He looked at Lisa with a faint smile. 'I wonder how long we *think* we've been conducting a normal conversation?'

She laughed softly. 'Quite some time. You've told me you love me three times today without moving your lips.'

He grinned. 'To think I took all that trouble to teach myself German and French.'

She touched his arm. 'Ursula has come to join us but I have an idea, let's call Dave Robinson.'

'What for?'

'Never mind, my dearest. Put it down to intuition if you like but let's call him.'

'As you wish.'

Robinson said: 'I'm a thousand miles away from you, what's the problem?'

Lisa laughed softly. 'No problem. We thought you'd like to meet a friend of ours, look through our eyes.'

There was no immediate response but, after a time: 'May I speak to her?'

'Sure, we'll fade out as soon as we've put you in touch.'

Lisa took Travers' arm. 'Let them get to know each other. I saw something curious by that tree over there.'

Half way to the tree, he said: 'What was it?' Then realization dawned. 'Women! You're match-making, aren't you?'

'Would you deny to others our kind of happiness?'

'Well, no, but—'

'I think I'm right, my darling, I have a feeling inside me.'

When they returned, Ursula's face was transfigured.

'Bless you.' She kissed Lisa's cheek. 'Bless you both. We must be together, I know you understand why. We cannot be apart now.'

'A thousand miles,' he reminded her gently, 'is the hell of a long way.'

'No, there is a way. Please, I have learned things from your minds which I did not know, watch, please.'

She stood still, smiling with happiness. 'Please watch.'

Travers realized suddenly that this tiny woman, less than five feet in height, had grown taller. Her face was now level with his own and then he saw that she was not taller. Her feet were clear of the ground.

'Levitation!'

She smiled. 'I don't know if it's levitation or controlled teleportation but I can fly to him. I have told him how to do it, so we shall meet half way. Thank you, my dear friends, we shall meet again soon.'

When she had gone, he said: 'Odd how one can miss out on a thing like that. My first experience of teleportation frightened me to death and I never considered slowing the process.'

'Yet Akron told us we could walk on water,' she said. 'We just didn't think.'

'Time and time again, I have to remind myself that to survive we *must* think.'

'You're worried, my darling.'

'Yes, I am.' He opened his mind fully to her and began to explain.

'Suppose we moved back in time a year, what would people think of humans like ourselves? Humans who could command the wind and tides. Humans who could teleport themselves from one side of the Earth to the other, who could heal the sick or kill by an effort of will? In time, they would come to regard us as Gods.'

He paused. 'We are *not* Gods, Lisa. We do not even feel like Gods yet God-like powers have been foisted upon us. What frightens me—and it frightened me from the first—is the fact that it's all too easy. How long before absolute power corrupts? How long before the moments of weakness and laziness grow longer and longer? A gardener, for example, who commands the ground to dig itself and the seeds to plant themselves in the prepared soil.

'At the moment, we are holding our own but it's precarious, too precarious for my peace of mind. Unless we watch it, we could become the instruments of our own destruction. We could become bloated, inert things, no longer human, let alone God-like. We could sit commanding our needs until we perish from sheer inertia.

'Already, many of our responsibilities have been lifted from us. True, this is a time of emergency, but aliens care for the world's children, but how long before we hand over everything to others? Unless we watch it, we could do exactly that.

'As I said earlier, we have the powers of Gods but we are not Gods. Yet, if we are to shoulder our responsibilities, we have to be exactly that. We have to be big enough, tough enough and wise enough to shoulder the burden.'

She clung to him, looking up into his face. 'My darling, I see it clearly. We share this problem but I, too, have to think.'

They walked on and she was silent for almost twenty minutes, then she said: 'The solution is not a happy one.'

'You have a solution?'

'I have the beginning of something, a few more minutes please. No, I think I can do this step by step.'

His arm tightened about her. 'Go ahead.'

'Well, when you first opened your mind to me, something which happened to you sort of stuck in my memory. You were aching and exhausted but you availed yourself of energy. You came to the conclusion that you had done no more than take a drink from a mountain stream.'

'Yes, I remember that clearly.'

'What I'm trying to say, dearest, is that we're not seeking someone like Akron or the other aliens to shoulder our responsibilities. We are seeking to shoulder them ourselves. Can we, with this in mind, avail ourselves of the strength and wisdom to do this? Couldn't we drink from another stream? After all, this thing, these faculties were sort of dumped on us.'

His face brightened. 'I think—maybe—no, I'm sure, you have the answer. We'll draw up a command between us, a most careful command—.'

It took them three hours before they were completely satisfied but they felt no change or results.

'I hope it worked,' she said a little worriedly.

Before he could answer, a telepathic thought touched their minds which they recognized instantly.

'Yes, Akron?'

'Congratulations, my friends, you are the first of your kind to reach for, and obtain, maturity.'

Three days later, they entered the children's settlement and, after a few hours rest, emerged on the opposite side.

He pointed. 'Over there, I got picked up by the Master's boys.'

She looked at the open land beyond the trees. A light mantle of snow hid the worst debris of the battle and even the burnt-out vehicles seemed less stark.

She stopped by a small tree and bent down. 'Look, snowdrops, the winter is nearly over.'

'Not quite,' he said. 'I'm referring to the flowers and not the season.'

'But they are, darling. I love flowers.'

'And they know it. Put your hand close to them again.'

She did so and her eyes widened. 'They're all leaning towards me!'

'Exactly,' he said, and laughed.

Four miles beyond the battlefield, Quade picked them up or, more aptly, he *failed* to pick them up. One of his patrols with field glasses had seen movement and reported the fact.

Quade looked through the man's eyes, saw two remote specks, probed telepathically and got nothing.

He was disturbed. Had the two specks been animals, there should have been some response. Complete negation, however, was beyond the scope of his experience.

Too many things had been happening lately for which he had been unable to find an explanation.

Recently there had been a detonation of such violence that cracks had appeared in several streets and four houses had completely collapsed. As the explosion had been four hundred miles away, he had been staggered by its force.

He conducted a quick search of the area and found a small group of wild horses some two hundred yards distant and looked through their eyes.

A man and a woman, outwardly ordinary, walking together unhurriedly, hand in hand.

He realized at once that they were by no means ordinary. It was not Spring yet but both wore light clothing in temperatures still well below freezing point. The man wore a half-sleeve shirt! The woman was quite beautiful and wore a sleeveless flowered blouse with—he was sure—damn all underneath it.

Their presence caused him more alarm than the explosion. In the first place, he couldn't read them and he couldn't *detect* them. In the second, it was obvious they had learned to adapt to extremes of temperature.

Where had they come from and where were they going? How had they got into his domain without triggering the alarms? Many had tried, he had disposed of two criminally-minded gentry only the previous day but they had been amateurs.

There was something about these two which bore the

stamp of the professional. They were adepts, he *felt* it.

His first reaction was to throw everything he had at them but caution restrained him. The worst thing he could do was to betray his presence.

In a case like this, a stab in the back was, by far, the best method. A gigantic bolt of energy might do the trick but, if it failed, they would immediately trace it to its source.

Quade undermined the ground directly in front of them to the depth of sixty feet. He left a covering of turf sufficiently thick to support itself without sagging. Once they stood on that, it would give way and they would plunge into the cavern below. He arranged some razor-sharp needles of rock for them to fall on.

The effort was in vain. The two simply changed direction and avoided the trap.

Judging by their expressions, they were not even aware there *was* a trap. There was no hesitation, no indication of alarm, they simply changed direction.

Quade tried the trap five times before he realized it was useless. They even changed direction *before* the trap was fully prepared.

There was no doubt now that they possessed a parapsychic defence far beyond anything he had yet met up with.

The knowledge alarmed him. Were these two unique or were there others? He couldn't let them go, he had to stay with them and learn all he could. He had to keep them under constant surveillance.

He withdrew his faculties from the horse and transferred them to a solitary bird.

It was a mistake.

Someone was already controlling the bird and had foreseen the possibility of a second party trying to take over. Something which felt like a heavy charge of electricity struck him inside his head. He staggered with a temporary but nearly intolerable migraine.

Quade had learned enough to realize that the two were not responsible but there were distinct ties. A friend —double friend? What the hell? had taken a quick look to make sure that all was well with them.

So there were others! Quade felt an unpleasant coldness in his stomach.

Another alarming thought arose. Someone had been watching him! For how long? Perhaps from the very beginning.

It was possible that these two were collaborators, perhaps they had formed some unholy alliance with the aliens behind the barrier. A barrier which, he admitted to himself, angrily, still defeated him completely.

Quade was a logical man. There was no one living, even in these days of parapsychic mastery, who did not possess an Achilles heel. It applied to himself, these two and to the aliens. He was going to find it. It was clearer than ever now that a showdown was inevitable. When it came, he was going to be ready.

The two were now approaching the main highway where months before, Travers had noted all the signs of panic. Mentally he braced them both for the desolate scenes of empty and now, no doubt, rusting vehicles.

It was not as he expected. True, some snow-covered wrecks remained but more than half had vanished as if they had never been.

Where they had stood were odd piles of remains, predominated by tyres.

'Upholstery,' he said, half to himself. 'Windshields, headlight glass, plastic instrument housing, floor carpets. It looks as if someone with an eye to business has been stripping this lot for the metal.'

'What about that one?' Lisa pointed. 'The blue limousine over there.'

'I see it, but it proves my point. Fibre-glass job, not much metal there.'

She glanced away and drew in her breath quickly. 'There's an old friend of yours down there.'

He looked in the direction she indicated and said: 'Well, well,' no longer frightened.

About half a mile down the highway, a bare ten feet above the surface, drifted the familiar disc.

He saw now that it was not a disc but, as he had at first supposed, a sphere. Due to some curious refraction of light, however, it still appeared to have a black rim.

Travers wondered if it contained aliens and probed it cautiously. He discovered it was a living creature, harmless unless attacked.

'It's a vulture,' he said cheerfully.

'A what?!'

He laughed. 'Sorry, love, having you on. It's an alien scavenger, only it doesn't eat decaying matter, it eats metal. Hence all the non-metal pieces left around.'

He grinned. 'It thinks it's in paradise from all I felt. Until it reached this world, metal was scarce and seldom on the surface.'

He helped her down the opposite bank of the highway. 'Way over there should be a blue van if our alien friend hasn't eaten it.'

They climbed a slight rise and he came to an abrupt stop.

'What the hell is that?'

About a quarter of a mile ahead of them was yet another sphere but this was on the ground and stood about sixty feet in height.

'It's alive,' he said after a few seconds, 'but it's not like our friend back there. It's a different kind of life altogether, let's take a closer look but cautiously.'

As they drew closer, she said: 'It's a pincushion with the pins pointing outwards.'

'Two-foot pins,' he observed. 'Hell, it's changing colour slowly. Look it's turning blue.'

'It isn't a sphere either,' she said quickly. 'It's a circle of trees folded over one another to form a sphere and they're straightening.'

They watched fascinated as the slender trees slowly straightened and become a beautiful pastel blue. White, star-shaped blossoms slowly appeared among the leaves.

'Defensive circle,' he said suddenly. 'Perhaps they heard our footsteps through the soil and they took defensive action until they knew we meant no harm.'

'They're intelligent.' She was probing gently. 'Not highly so but equal to a dog, empathic too and they're sort of pleased to see us.'

They approached closer and in the centre of the circle they could see a number of delicate blue shoots.

'They were protecting their young,' she said wonderingly. She reached up and touched one of the blue leaves. 'It's warm! Can you have a warm-blooded plant or should it be a warm-chlorophylled plant?'

He laughed. 'This is an alien lifeform, it doesn't have to conform to our understanding of what is a plant and what isn't.'

They walked on and ten minutes later, he pointed. 'The van, you can just see the roof.'

As Travers had anticipated, Beamish had not survived his 'death ray'. What remained of him was half covered in snow, pine needles and dead leaves.

There was a bare patch of ground, clear of snow, where he had last seen the weapon but it was no longer there. His faculties conveyed the impression that it had somehow broken down and been absorbed by the soil.

It occurred to him that this might change the chemical character of the ground in the immediate area. Here, perhaps, alien seeds would take root. On the other hand, plant and insect life natural to Earth in the immediate area might also suffer change.

He put his arm round Lisa and held her closer.

She knew what he was thinking and feeling, she was part of him.

'I know,' she said. 'The Earth we love is changing and often I feel close to tears, too. Often one longs for familiar things despite their shortcomings. I think of the great cities crumbling and falling to ruin. I think of the mines empty, the railroads overgrown and the factories rusting. I dream of all the liners and freighters, now just hulks wallowing in empty oceans—.'

Quade had relinquished his watch for the time being, he could not afford to waste time.

His previous assurance had vanished completely. He could have conquered the past world but not the present one.

In the first place, his recent discovery of the two adepts had jolted him into making a world survey.

It was not an encouraging picture. There were other set-ups like his own in various parts of the world.

A vicious opportunist with an ice-cold mind had Eastern Europe tied down tight in a parapsychic prison which made previous police states anywhere look like rest homes.

An ex-convict controlled most of Mexico, an intelligent pervert, most of Southern England—.

Quade went through the lot. Six were formidable and dangerous, five dangerous but vulnerable and eighteen push-overs. All he could say now was that he was master of Canada.

He went to his desk and collected some papers. He had, he remembered undertaken a breakdown on survival in the early days of this business.

His figures brought him no comfort. There were sixteen million survivors unaccounted for. As Quade had arrived at these figures by dead reckoning based on local observation and data, it was a startling mathematical survey. He had estimated that the world's total population would stabilize at ninety million and he was three hundred and twenty thousand out on his estimate.

He was, however, concentrating on the missing sixteen million. He had evidence that they existed, camp sites and so on, but that was all—they were *undetectable*.

He spent several days using his faculties indirectly but with considerable caution. He had learned to his cost that some entities in the universe were extremely touchy about their telepathic wave-lengths. Most, at first contact, put up a barrier but there were those who slapped him off as a warning.

A telepathic slap was not pleasant. It was like an accurately placed right hook to the inside of his head and made him feel sick for several minutes.

There were others in which withering contempt or downright revulsion were almost palpable. They left him with the uneasy feeling that he stank.

He found it necessary to revise his thinking and realized he had missed many lessons when the Master had brought about his own defeat.

No matter how many ultra-sophisticated weapons he filched, they were still *natural* weapons.

He went through his armoury in his mind. He had a bomb, no bigger than an egg, which, if introduced into a city the size of New York, would leave only a smoking crater. He had side-arms capable of stopping an armoured division. A missile, so exact, it would knock a cigarette out of man's mouth on the other side of the world.

He saw now that all these terrifying weapons had their limitations. The super bomb could not only be deflected but bounced right back at him by the simple command of an adept.

He could, of course, bounce it right back again but that sort of attrition got you nowhere.

He *had* to get something to rub out those adepts and, if he could get that, he could deal with the rest in his own time.

It took him five days. A great deal of it at the cost of considerable mental effort which left him exhausted. Somehow, a great many things failed to arrive with the same ease as in the past.

It had never occurred to him that even faculties have limits, that the mechanism in his mind could be overworked to the point of atrophy.

Whereas the wise, like Travers and his friends, had used restraint, Quade had overworked his powers prodigiously and invariably for his own ends.

Construction of the weapon, took a further five days but he was confident of his success.

He had what he was pleased to call a parapsychic mechanical weapon—beyond the normal man's imagining. It owed nothing to this world, it had been conceived and executed in a different time/space. Only its actual construction had taken place on Earth. Now, at last, he was ready. It would be interesting indeed to see how those two cocksure adepts would handle this.

## CHAPTER NINE

The two had just crossed the secondary highway and Travers was pointing.

'There's my car, you can just see the roof. I could get no closer, there was—.'

He never finished the sentence. It was as if something had taken over his body and triggered his reflexes into action.

They were standing about six feet apart, he dived for her legs and brought her down on the top of him. He twisted his body frantically and they both rolled down the slight rise on which they had been standing.

Intense heat rushed above them and, where they had been standing, about twenty feet of soil puffed upwards in white ash.

He didn't say: 'Don't crawl away, crawl forward, follow the rise.' In an emergency, they acted and thought as one although the initiative came from him.

Past experience was helping him now. An attacker would reason that they would use the undulating ground as a cover for escape, not as a means of edging forward.

'There's nothing there,' she said. She was frightened but she could draw strength from him mentally.

'Nothing we can detect, it's shielded.' He raised his head quickly then hastily ducked down. 'It's invisible but there's a slight distortion between two trees over there. Whatever it is, it must generate a certain amount of heat.'

'Quade?'

'Yes, he's watching.' Then, quickly, 'Check the sky.'

She blacked-out a high flying bird and, in his study, Quade swore.

However, his specialist instrument could act on its own initiative and should now be moving forward. All he had to do was to sit and wait.

Travers and Lisa realized that they were pitted against the extraordinary and were sending out distress signals. They were not inactive, however, they lowered the atmospheric temperature to sub-zero levels between themselves and the trees.

'I can see the bastard,' he said savagely. 'The distortion is more pronounced now.'

He lifted a rampart of earth thirty feet high in front of it and they sprinted to a hollow even closer.

It was then that thirty thousand adepts in answer to their distress calls concentrated all their power on Quade's instrument of destruction.

When the rampart of earth rose before it, the weapon transferred itself to the top, at which instant, the appeal for help was responded to.

Quade's lack of imagination became immediately apparent. He had never visualized an attack by thousands. The parapsychic shielding plus the invisibility circuits had never been designed to withstand such concentrated force and both failed together.

For exactly six seconds, Quade's weapon became visible. An oddly ribbed metallic football poised on six spidery legs. The legs were bent as if the creature was about to spring. Then, abruptly the legs turned cherry-red and broke in several places. The football-shaped body toppled sideways, melting and puffs of steam rose up from the snow as it dripped metal and lost shape. Then, without warning, a thin jet of vapour hissed upwards and it was gone.

The two rose from the hollow and he put his arm round her shoulders.

'You're not hurt, my love?'

'Hurt, no, but a bit shaky.'

He held her closer. 'I know. I'm not exactly calm myself. Guess we'd better thank our friends.'

In his study, Quade held his head. He knew what had happened because he felt the repercussions in himself.

It was not, however, the end of the business, not for Quade. As he made to rise from his chair, it seemed as if a grenade had exploded inside his head. He realized later that the contact was deliberately brutalized as a warning but, at the time, he staggered and moaned.

*'Quade, you're an amateur and a blundering amateur at that. In future, therefore, keep your ambitions to yourself or the next time we shall burn you up—clear?*

*'We are forming a free society, Quade, therefore you are free to do as you choose. You leave our people alone.*

*'We could point out the consequences of your actions but it would be a waste of time.*

*'However, we should be failing in our duty if we did not point out your position at this moment in time. You still have the chance to join us.*

*'Stop and think before you reject the proposal. We can give you every help.*

*'Think, Quade. We must warn you now that when you begin to reap what you have sown with such profligate disregard for the new laws which now prevail, it will be too late.*

*'We repeat. It will be too late. When that time comes, neither we nor any other power in the universe can help you.'*

The telepathic message was of such force that for hours Quade could do nothing but strive for peace of mind. He was, he knew, close to anxiety neurosis. Abject terror and strange but elusive apprehensions surged through his mind.

His supposedly impregnable defences had been penetrated with insulting ease. He had not been 'open' but the telepathic warning had come close to mentally disembowelling him.

His brain surged with questions. What had he sown which he must ultimately reap? What were the signs he would see and just how would it be too late?

Quade knew there was one escape route. Enlisting the proffered help, he could change his character and place himself in the opposite camp. He knew this on an intellectual level but he was psychologically incapable of taking advantage of it.

Again on an intellectual level, he knew he was like a

man in a monkey trap. All he had to do was open his hand but, in order to escape, he must release what he had grasped.

He *couldn't* let go. Power was essential to him, power and the things it provided. He liked the pleasure it gave him, the absolute mastery over others. The cherished orgies in which the young women vied with each other to obey his most obscene whims.

He liked his enslaved followers prostrating themselves before him and, in the summing up, he couldn't stop playing God. All his life he had longed for this, now it was his and he couldn't relinquish it.

Travers and Lisa reached the dirt road in early Spring. They had sixty miles to go but they had calls to make en route.

The three cars were still there but no longer gleaming. Frost, snow and bird droppings had taken the shine but none showed signs of rust.

Travers felt sadness and nostalgia. He loved cars and loved driving for the love of driving.

'I wonder if they'll start. The keys are still in them.'

All three started at the first attempt which made him even sadder. What a waste of magnificent machines and inspired engineering. He was going to miss driving like hell—why should he? Why, when things were straightened out, couldn't he come back for one of these?

With the thought, a whole series of new ideas came tumbling into his mind and he kissed Lisa unexpectedly full on the lips.

'Darling, listen, I've hit something. A question has been

at the back of my mind for months and now, quite by accident, I think I've found the answer. Look, we're trying to form a stable culture but to achieve that we have to have *balance*.'

He laughed boyishly and continued. 'We've both been visualising a society where everything is finished and all the past is dead but it isn't and never can be. I want to drive that Rolls but I'll lay odds of a hundred to one that there are those among us whose hands would be twitching at the first sight of it. People who love machines and doing things with their hands.

'There are architects who love designing buildings and people who like constructing. Artists will still want to paint, composers produce music which musicians will still want to play.

'Our technological society is not finished, cities will rise again. We shall not be a pastoral society with parapsychic powers. We shall be a *balanced* society for our natures are such that we shall strike a compromise. There will always be those among us who want to *do* things and only through *doing* things themselves can they find true fulfilment.'

She smiled up at him, aware of the truth of his words and sharing his happiness.

Ten minutes later, they found Alcott, the man who had once thought he was God.

He stood on a tall rock, arms folded, feet slightly apart, chin raised commandingly but he was quite dead.

Travers touched the hem of the theatrical cloak and found it was stone. The entire body was stone.

Somehow, somewhere, 'God' had gone wrong on a command and perpetuated himself in granite uselessness.

'Look on my works, ye mighty, and despair,' Travers quoted half to himself.

She nodded. 'Shelley isn't it? I know that line, most appropriately.'

They came to the web which had once so terrified him. It still spanned the entire clearing but no longer shimmered with rainbows. It was as dull as rusty wire and, to the touch, as brittle as glass.

In the centre of the clearing they found the remains of the thing which had once spun the web. There was a sort of shell, maybe ten feet across but now perforated in many places. There was a sort of skull, with eye sockets six inches in diameter but that was all.

The spider—if spider it had been—had not survived long on Earth.

The bright Spring, however, quickly showed them that other lifeforms had been more fortunate.

There were large areas of pastel blue grass and they came upon a low growth which had fitted itself snugly into earth ecology. It had soft orange-coloured leaves and delicate white flowers. The early bees appeared unaware of its alien origin and were busily collecting nectar.

Later they saw some purple insects with long green wings doing exactly the same job on some natural earth blossoms.

In the sky crows wheeled, some wild duck in V-formation but below them, as big as the ducks, two odd-looking balls of yellow fluff supported themselves on swiftly beating transparent wings.

A solitary hawk swooped for a cursory examination, then turned away. These strange creatures, too, seemed to have adapted themselves swiftly to their new environment.

They came to a small lake and he grinned. 'What about it?'

'It looks wonderful.'

They stripped and plunged in.

Afterwards they sat on the edge of the lake talking and while they sat there, something came out of the trees and stood watching them.

They knew it was there but did not turn. They could *feel* it was nervous but anxious to be friendly. It wasn't human but it had a level of intelligence far above that of any Earth animal.

After a time, it put one foot carefully before the other and came forward a few paces.

They already knew it was telepathically responsive but were restraining their faculties for fear of alarming it.

To Lisa, although she knew it was alien, it had certain familiarities which abruptly fell into place. Once months ago, she had scouted ahead for danger through the eyes of a—.

'It's a dog,' she said. 'It may not look like a dog but there are a lot of similarities.'

'It's lonely,' he acknowledged. 'It needs companionship and, yes, it has the same capacity for devotion. You could be right.'

The thing which felt like a dog took a few more paces but delicately and poised for flight.

It did not reason on the same lines as a man but used two of its most efficient faculties to determine the nature of the creatures by the water—empathy and smell.

It decided they felt nice and their smell, although strange, was not repellent. They were not like the savage thing he had met in the mountains. A brown thing which had stood on its hind legs and tried to slash him.

He came a little closer and sat down just behind them. He was now satisfied that here was no tendency to violence.

Proximity brought him further information. In the first place, they were love-mate. In the second, and more important, here was an age-old affinity with animals. It had not been so on his home world where, although there had been no ill-treatment, there was alas, little real understanding.

The animal was fortunate. It had been drawn to Earth by the half-command of a drunken seaman who had beaten his previous dog to death. At almost the same instant, the seaman wished himself back at sea. The loose command dumped the sailor exactly where he wanted—in the middle of the Pacific. There was no vessel, the drunken wish had specified no vessel.

As the animal seated itself, they could see its reflection in the clear waters of the lake.

Travers gave a low-key, telepathic 'Good God!'

The alien animal was obviously and unmistakably a dog—if you were prepared to accept a dog nearly as big as a pony. It was covered in woolly green fur and had huge, untidy-looking droopy ears.

Travers said: 'Hello, old fellow,' cautiously.

The dog stood up and wagged its huge hairy tail slowly, now inwardly determined to stick. It *liked* these two creatures.

He licked Lisa's naked back with a tongue as big as a hand towel to show he meant well.

Lisa stood up and patted his head. 'I shall call him Obadiah,' she said.

'You'll call him what? Good God!' He laughed. 'You won't, you know. Within ten minutes the name will be too damn long and you'll call him Obar. You intend to keep it?'

'It's already stuck to us, you must feel it.'

'Yes, I know.' He made wider contact and was staggered at the level of intelligence. Obadiah could count up to ten and had the approximate, although off-beat, intelligence of an eight year old child.

To his surprise, the dog didn't eat although it drank frequently. Somewhere in the course of evolution, although jaws and teeth had been retained, nature had provided another form of sustenance.

There was a wide band of silver coloured fur on the animal's back which absorbed sunlight. This energy was converted into food although Travers was unable to understand the marvellous chemistry which made it possible.

'Well it's house-trained anyway,' he said. 'I wonder if it likes a game.'

Obadiah did. He plunged into the lake when Lisa threw a stick into the water with an enormous splash and conveyed a feeling of utter delight.

When he came out, he shook himself and drenched them both.

'Keep clear of his tail when he's happy,' said Travers. 'It looks capable of knocking down a small tree.'

Travers, although he had correctly estimated the animal's intelligence, was amazed at the way it responded to casual training.

Obadiah only needed a command to be illustrated once and his intelligence and empathic sense made it stick. The dog not only obeyed but quickly grasped the reason for obedience. Commands were for his own protection as well as theirs. They didn't say 'come', 'heel', 'freeze' or 'lie down' for amusement. If one of them said 'freeze' it was because the safety of all might depend on that single command.

Obadiah took upon himself the authority of a dog—he had taken all the mental pictures from their minds while they trained him. He knew, therefore, that dogs were not only beloved companions, they were also protectors. They guarded their owners' persons and property.

Obadiah, radiating detectable inner happiness, scouted ahead importantly. He had found his rightful place on this strange world and he was happy in it.

The inn looked slightly dilapidated when they reached it but inside someone had tidied up thoughtfully. The remains of Wallace had been removed from the bar, the floors swept and all rubbish removed.

'Pabst,' said Travers, smiling. 'I can detect his presence—hey, wait a minute, he wasn't alone, he's found someone.'

'I feel that too,' she said. 'I'm so happy for him. That makes three of us, doesn't it?'

He laughed. 'Six to make three, screwy mathematics.'

He dropped into one of the large chairs. 'Make some room for my feet, Obar, damn you.'

Obadiah thumped his huge tail on the floor and moved precisely two inches. He was fully aware that there was no force behind the words.

An hour later Akron arrived. 'At our last meeting, I hinted at important news but I must wait for the others, they will be here soon.'

Pabst arrived first with a slender fair haired woman who he introduced as Greta.

He anticipated Travers' question. 'Yes, I know she looks appropriately Teutonic but actually she's Swedish, not that nationalities matter now. By the way, Nasuki will be along soon. He too is lucky but in this case it's a girl of his own race—'

He was interrupted by the arrival of Robinson and Ursula. Nasuki arrived five minutes later with a tiny slant-eyed girl whose name none of them were able to pronounce verbally.

'I've been cradle snatching.' He grinned. 'No deceit, she knows I was once ninety-two.'

When they were all comfortably seated, Akron said: 'Your minds, as usual, bubble with questions but in none do I detect the most important of all. That question is, "how did we come to be as we are?" You have reached only a part conclusion on this subject—an infection. I will now describe the infection and how it was introduced to Earth—.'

When he had finished, they were all silent for some seconds.

Finally Pabst said: 'Germ warfare, eh? And this furry despot is still on his way here?'

'In about eighteen months, assuming he does not pay for his blunder which is more than possible.'

He paused and the evasive face appeared to smile. 'I find a certain ironic humour in the situation. An invader arrives expecting dead sheep and is confronted by live tigers. One of you, any single one, could tear his immense fleet to pieces like so many cardboard toys. A single casual thought could prime and detonate every solar bomb his ships carry. Small combustible substances could be introduced into the highly unstable converter tubes which drive his vessels.'

He paused again. 'But you will not do this, you are achieving maturity rapidly.'

'May I ask a rather pointed question?' Robinson had half risen from his chair.

'Certainly.'

'Well this may sound rude but I hope you won't take it that way. I've heard a lot lately about maturity and mature races. What were these mature races doing when this joker was throwing missiles at us?'

'A sensible question, Mr Robinson, and the answer is—*abiding by the rules*. The rules are that under no circumstances may a mature race interfere in any way whatever with the growth of an immature culture. In your case, we believe this happened but we will come to that later.'

It was Lisa who asked the vital question.

'How did this biochemical infection make us parapsychic?'

Akron dropped his bombshell quietly and without drama. 'It didn't—*you were always parapsychic.*'

They were silent, looking at one another uneasily.

'The entire race of man?' asked Ursula.

'The entire race of man.' Akron leaned forward slightly.

'You must understand that someone, some race unknown, broke the rules which I have just mentioned and interfered with an immature culture. They came to Earth at the dawn of your history and inhibited your faculties. No doubt there was some genetic manipulation as well to make sure the inhibitions were passed on with each successive generation. However, to simplify, at some early period in your history, some unscrupulous intelligence came to your planet and virtually blindfolded your entire race.'

The picture suddenly fell into place in Travers' mind. 'I get it! When that infection hit us, it failed not only to kill us but it only attacked that part of our brains which inhibited our faculties.'

'Exactly so, *it removed the blindfold.*'

'Why?' asked Lisa, quietly. 'Why should a supposedly mature race do a thing like that to us?'

Akron conveyed sadness. 'There can be but one answer. They saw in your ultimate growth, a threat to their power in the universe. They therefore chose to arrange things so that you would never pose a danger to them.'

'But a mature race!' said Pabst angrily.

'No,' said Akron firmly. 'A race of great deceivers who have come close to achieving the impossible by fooling all of the people all of the time.'

'Who?' asked Pabst. 'Just which race did this?'

'That we have yet to determine. It will take time but we shall succeed.'

'And having succeeded, can we prove it?'

'Not yet. Not in the eyes of those who will finally judge.'

'Why didn't these things just knock us off?' enquired Travers angrily. 'Just one super bomb in the right place would have done the trick.'

'Again, the rules. The obliteration of an entire culture would have meant a major and searching enquiry. Therefore this had to be done by stealth and by methods which betrayed no outward change.'

'I take it that the same race were responsible for the explosion,' said Lisa.

'True, but anti-matter impulses travel far in excess of light speeds and leave no trace as to their point of origin. Rest assured, however, the perpetrators dare not repeat such an attack. The universe is alert now and preparations for such an assault would immediately be detected.'

He paused and conveyed a sad smile. 'You appreciate, I hope, that socially, you have split the universe from end to end.'

Travers could. It was like a thousand honest people suddenly discovering that there was a thief among them. Suspicion would fall on all until the culprit was detected. Further, each one would have doubts about the others and distrust must be building up fast.

It was Pabst who asked the leading question. 'How many races have the necessary technology for an anti-matter impulse? Before you answer that question, couple it with this one. How many races have been around long enough to parapsychically blindfold us when we still may have been on all fours?'

Akron conveyed respect. 'A shrewd and highly penetrating question. I am beginning to understand why a race of deceivers preferred to render you impotent.'

He paused and shook his head. 'I can think of only ten.'

'Well that narrows it down somewhat.'

'Very true, but it is better that you have some understanding of the opposition. Six of these races are parapsychic, the remaining four have raised their technology to such inspired heights that they equal in terms of power, the remainder. The Empires of all ten span several galaxies and all have been active in the universe long before your sun and its solar system came into being.'

'Thanks,' said Pabst, sourly. 'I call that cheering news.'

'Do not become despondent. You are not alone, the entire universe is as anxious to expose the culprit as yourselves. At the moment—please don't take the idiom literally, some don't have any—there are many red faces in the universe. One of their number has conned them, an impostor has been among them almost since the birth of history and remained undetected.'

'You said something about a final test,' said Travers.

'Yes, I have taken the liberty of calling the greatest known expert to conduct this test. I trust you have no objections?'

'None whatever.'

'Think before you answer, please, since the subject on which he will conduct the tests will be you.'

'Eh? Sorry. What does he want me to do?'

'He wants to open your mind so that he can read your racial memories.'

'Is it dangerous?' enquired Lisa, suddenly tense.

'No. On that you have my solemn word but, on the other hand, it could be distinctly unpleasant. You see, Mr

Travers will re-live a brief period of one of his remotest ancestors' lives. Subjectively he will go back in time, many millions of years in time. He will go back to the period when an unknown intelligence placed a blindfold on his people's faculties.'

## CHAPTER TEN

'When does he arrive?' asked Travers.

'Within the hour. In the meantime, I have here the summary of a report on your culture arrived at by a committee of experts—'

*'The stunted cultural and social development of the Human Race measured against its racing technology may only be explained psychologically. The race is over-compensating for deficiency of which it is half aware.*

*'To appreciate this half awareness, it is necessary only to study the culture a short time. Infant, juvenile and adult literature abound with parapsychic references. Infant literature of 'magical' events to the super beings of adolescent adventure stories.*

*'The culture's major religions come close to being founded upon parapsychic phenomena and most certainly upon those reputedly able to demonstrate it.*

*'The ills, excesses and conflicts which have plagued this race result from one cause only—a desperate striving to regain its birthright.'*

Akron stopped. Then he said: 'This report has deeply impressed every intelligence in the universe. The final test confirms beyond doubt—'

The expert, when he arrived, contrived to look more human than Akron.

He had a human, gentle although wholly expressionless face. He told them his name was Grayle.

'Please sit down, Mr Travers—ah, yes, I see the position, your female complement must remain linked to you telepathically.'

Lisa, who was slightly over-wrought, suppressed a giggle with an effort. Being called a female complement was something new.

'How will you know when you strike the right period?' asked Travers.

'A fairly simple procedure. There will be a marked break in continuity. Racial memory forgets nothing, you must understand and, as you must know, occasionally surfaces. The person who says "I have been here before" or quotes incidents in a past life, is merely drawing on his racial memories. Now, if you will be good enough to open your mind, please—.'

Travers did so and as Travers he ceased to exist.

He had no name. The small tribe did not bestow names. One recognized one's fellows emphatically or by sense of smell. In this primitive society, body odour was more distinctive than features.

The man-thing, Travers' remote ancestor, was smelly, unwashed and content.

Verdant jungle covered the land masses of the Earth but, in view of what came later, it was neutral rather than hostile.

The danger came from the earth itself for, all too frequently, it opened in a great crevasse and great sections of earth and jungle disappeared into the opening. Sometimes it snapped shut again with a noise like thunder or it just lay open exhaling choking smoke and shimmering heat. Then the trees on either side would crisp and burst into flame.

Sometimes the earth would just burst open and a jet of roaring flame or steam would rush upwards.

The man-thing had never seen the sun or, for that matter, the tops of the trees for the Earth was swathed in mist. Almost continuous rain ensured that it seldom lifted and visibility varied from a few feet to a few yards.

Climate should have been tropical but volcanic action raised daily temperatures almost to oven level.

A fair amount of ultra-violet managed to penetrate the cloud and mist and where the man-thing wasn't hairy, he was brown. He was also stark naked but this, to a casual observer, would have mattered little. He was hairy enough to be fully clothed.

Water ran off the hair and sweat out of it and the creature scratched frequently. It had a flat, wide-nostrilled face, little black eyes and looked stupid.

Stupidity, however is a relative word. The life-expectation of a creature with ten times the intelligence in that jungle could be accurately assessed at twenty minutes.

The man-thing could make guttural noises but had no language. It had developed no weapons but controlled its environment. It also had a built-in faculty for danger. It 'felt' some hours before, when the thundering mountain was going to roll its waves of molten rock into the jungle.

It knew, days before, when its particular area was going to be buried in several feet of ash and pumice.

There were, of course, things in the jungle which hissed like geysers and shook the earth when they moved but the man-thing was not afraid of these. He would deceive or frighten them. Usually he preferred to deceive, fear was not an emotion he cared for himself.

It was not hard to deceive the creatures by playing on their senses. Then they would go crashing away in the opposite direction after a prey which they believed to be directly in front of them.

As the man-thing moved onwards unhurriedly, it grunted to itself, first loudly then quietly until the grunts became a pattern. It was happy and this was equivalent of singing.

After a short time it stopped and reached towards the middle of its back, first with one hand and then with the other. Then it blew through its lips with an unmistakable grimace of exasperation. One of the local parasites was having a meal just where he was unable to reach it.

There were counter-measures for this situation. He fumbled in the hair on his belly and withdrew a lizard. The lizard was about two inches long and bright blue. It was one of four he carried about his person.

He placed the lizard on his shoulder and it immediately disappeared into the hair.

After a brief period an expression of beatific relief appeared in the man-thing's eyes. The lizard had found the offending parasite, devoured it and obligingly scratched.

The man-thing had established an empathic rapport with the lizards and a highly efficient symbiosis was developing. It was a rewarding relationship for all concerned. The lizards dealt with parasites and scratched him where he itched. In return, they received protection, free transport and an abundance of their natural diet.

The man-thing continued onwards for about a mile and then turned abruptly right. Its faculties had warned it of danger and it had taken evasive action.

Thirty minutes later on its previous route, twelve trees were suddenly hurled high in the air. They were followed by a hail of rock and soil and a roaring column of incandescent gas.

The heat was so intense that, for fifty yards on either side, the jungle immediately withered and burst into flame.

Two hours later he rejoined his small tribe and was immediately aware of disturbance.

He was shocked to discover that of the eighteen males and twenty-three females, he recognized not a single one empathically.

He was compelled to smell them all, including the twelve infants, in order to assure himself of their identity. The smell also informed him that they were alarmed—for him fear had a bitter and acrid smell.

His mate took his hand and tugged, clearly urging him to follow. She led him to a mound of dried lava and, there, on the top of it was the machine.

He did not recognize it as a machine, to him it was a square rock.

The 'rock' was full of round holes through which coloured lights were visible and it made an odd high-pitched humming.

The humming seemed to go right inside his head and he put his fingers in his ears to try and keep it out. His fingers made no difference because the humming in his head just went on.

He was frightened and ran away. An hour later he discovered that he had lost contact with his lizards. He could find them with his hands but that was all.

While he stood there puzzling, the earth opened and closed like the jaws of a trap. It swallowed four of his tribe completely and fear clutched at his stomach. Why hadn't the tribe known it was coming? Why hadn't *he* known?

He realized slowly—although he could never have expressed it wholly—that somehow the jungle and his familiar world had changed from the neutral to the hostile.

Slowly the man-thing seemed to fade away and Travers was Travers again.

Grayle said: 'Most informative. This final evidence places the matter beyond dispute. However, as additional evidence, can you describe this box in greater detail?'

Travers frowned. 'It looked metallic, dull green in colour. It stood about a foot high and was about double that in length. Let's see now, I can't recall how many holes.'

'Eight,' said Lisa, quickly. 'They were about an inch from the top.'

'They were about a quarter of an inch in diameter and the lights seemed to stab out for several feet.'

'Anything else, please?'

'Yes, there was a sort of black stud in the lower right hand corner. Could have been a retaining screw or a seal but I remember it was nonreflective.'

Grayle nodded. 'I would personally conclude it was a time mechanism. It is logical to assume that the instrument would self-destruct once its purpose was fulfilled thus leaving no evidence.'

'What now?' asked Robinson.

'With this conclusive evidence, the committee will institute a thorough investigation.'

'How long will that take?'

'It may take several years.'

Travers frowned. 'Time enough for them to cook up something new and different. Such a delay could be dangerous for us.'

'That is true but the entire universe is on watch for you.'

'All but one and a very smart one at that.'

'Procedure must be followed,' said Grayle gently.

'With respect, the committee must follow procedure but we don't have to.'

'You have ideas of your own?' enquired Akron.

'Yes. Probably you'll find them pretty crude but they have certain secondary merits which the intelligences in the universe might welcome.'

'We are open to suggestions,' said Akron politely.

'Thank you. You will recall then, in an earlier conversation we narrowed the field of possible perpetrators to ten?'

'Yes.'

'In which case,' said Travers harshly, 'speaking for myself and all those present, I'd make damn sure that every race in the universe knew the names of those ten. This, from your point of view as an outworlder, would remove a great deal of distrust from a vast number of races.'

Akron appeared to nod. 'It is crude but I concede the merits.'

'It is also highly provocative,' said Grayle.

'It is intended to be,' said Pabst. 'Further, pressure will be concentrated on the ten suspects and not dissipated by uncertainty and distrust. It is even possible that some of the innocent will come forward to prove it, thus narrowing the field even more.'

'It is most unorthodox,' said Grayle. 'The committee will veto it immediately.'

It seemed to Travers that Grayle's mental voice lacked force and there were detectable undertones of approval.

'We are not members of the committee,' pointed out Nasuki reasonably. 'Therefore we are not answerable to it.'

'Correct.' It was evident that Akron had made up his mind. 'I will co-operate in this scheme. Speaking for myself, I will see that the names of the ten suspects are disseminated widely.'

Grayle bowed. 'I have many reservations but I will do the same—.'

Spring had come to Canada, save for one area, for Quade was beginning to reap what he had sown.

Among his enslaved thousands was a man named Andrew Keen. He was an average sort of man who had once been a skilled maintenance worker in a large engineering concern.

Somehow Keen had survived the first few days and learned a command word from sheer necessity. Once that was acquired, however, he had been too timorous to experiment or continue further.

The command made him safe. He liked to feel safe. Providing he minded his own business and didn't play about with whatever it was he had, he should remain safe.

He wandered the countryside, living from hand to mouth until Quade roped him in.

Quade gave him *security.* Quade gave him a feeling of normality, directing him to jobs where he could use his hands. True, a lot of the jobs concerned strange machines, and weird sorts of weapons but the work gave him stability.

Quade had restored order, lights in the streets, transport and civilized living.

Quade protected him and, in return, Keen worshipped him. When not working, he loitered in the streets, as did many others, hoping that Quade would pass.

If he did, he would prostrate himself and yearn for notice or the blessing of a smile.

In the last few weeks, Keen had been aware of other things which disturbed him.

He knew, by the position of the sun, that it was Spring but why had not Spring come to this city? Ice still clung to wall and roof and icy winds howled through the streets.

It was true that the sun was visible but it looked smaller, more remote and somehow contained a hint of shadow.

The factor which had upset him the most, however, was the appearance of the Krull. No one knew where the name originated but the name stuck because it seemed to fit.

Quade had cleansed the city of rats from the beginning but now the Krull had come to take their place.

The Krull resembled a tail-less lobster and gave off a sour and penetrating odour. They were a dirty white in colour and had glowing, bright pink eyes on short stalks. Like the lobster, they had long, slender antennae which were in constant motion.

In the few short weeks of Spring they had become a plague. They scuttled about floors with a disturbing scraping noise. They walked up walls and across ceilings from whence, all too often, they fell.

They were difficult to kill for their shells were hard and many had learned to their cost that they could bite painfully.

Keen shared a secret fear with many others that a lot of them would one day catch him alone and attack. He was terrified that one would fall from the ceiling and onto his bed while he slept. In any case he lost such sleep from their continuous scraping and gnawing for they were eating the houses to pieces.

Keen admitted to himself that he didn't feel right and too often he caught himself on the verge of blasphemy. He'd caught himself more than once thinking that Quade was a nasty little man with a paunch.

It was odd how the one-time feeling of protection had become suffocating.

Keen sat down and thought about it and suddenly he wanted to get away.

Almost without thinking, he gave the command word 'I want to get out of this city.'

It was as if a dark shutter had snapped open in his mind and he saw his way clear. There was nothing to it. All he had to do was to walk out.

No one would stop him or question him. No one would think he would *want* to leave.

Fifteen minutes later he was on his way but somehow his vision had changed. He saw the city from a new viewpoint and too many defects had now become visible.

Strange-looking oily grey moss was growing in great splotches on many walls and in many corners. In open ground, new shoots were rising from the soil but not green shoots—black shoots with barbs like fish hooks.

He thought it strange he had not noticed these things before and, as for Quade, how the hell had he come to worship a man like that?

Keen reached the limits of the city and set out across country but within twenty minutes something touched his mind.

'Do not be afraid. I am a friend. Keep walking straight ahead.'

The words in his mind felt friendly, brought assurance and there was no underlying hint of coercion such as he had experienced with Quade.

Presently he saw someone leaning against a tree. At first he thought it was a man, then a woman and then he saw it was two people, a man and a slender fair haired woman.

The man who was big and jovial came forward, hand extended.

'Hello, Mr Keen, I've been waiting for you. My name is Pabst—.'

Quade had lost forty-three men and thirty-eight women before he discovered it.

He was not to know that the same thing was happening in basically similar set-ups all over the world. The inherently decent were finding the strength within themselves to get out from under.

Quade realized with each passing day that, apart from killing them, there was nothing he could do about it. The exodus had begun in twos and threes but, within a week, had increased to tens and twenties.

Dimly he began to see his deficiencies. One could not go on taking without putting something in. It had a parallel with agriculture. One had to let the land lie fallow or feed it on a massive scale, otherwise the crops became more stunted and inferior with each passing season.

Figuratively speaking, Quade had no fertilizer, manure or nitrates and the equivalent of leaving the land fallow would render him defenceless.

Other things disturbed him. Spring had come beyond his area of control but not within it.

The dark moss which Keen had noticed had now appeared again within a few hours and gained a wider hold.

Frighteningly, he was unable to dispel it and it came to him that it was a by-product or side-effect of the misuse of his own faculties.

So were the leafless vines which now flourished on every patch of open soil. They could be cut or burned down but began to grow again almost immediately. They were protected by wickedly hooked barbs which could inflict nasty wounds on the careless.

The Krull, he appreciated, were of alien origin and some had been brought in with the many things he had filched while at the height of his parapsychic powers. These powers had now deteriorated to such an extent that he could not remove them. Intellectually and resentfully, he was forced to acknowledge that these things could only flourish in his kind of set-up.

Quade looked up at the sun, knowing that the absence of heat was due to his own lack of foresight. So anxious had he been to erect an impenetrable canopy over his domain which would resist *every* conceivable force including heat that it repelled the heat of the sun. Ice still clung to walls and streets and there was an invading chill to which he was unable to adapt.

His followers, losing their enthusiasm rapidly, went about their business huddled up in several overcoats. Outdoor work resulted in empty buildings being plundered for inflammable materials. Huge fires were built at intersections which invariably resulted in huge palls of black smoke, very little flame and even less heat.

Each day the sun seemed more remote than ever and the shadows more pronounced.

The exodus continued. In the course of three weeks, a community of two hundred and twenty-eight thousand had dwindled to nine thousand.

The telepathic warning came back to him with renewed force. '*When you begin to reap what you have sown, it will be too late.*'

Terror seized him. He had to get away. He had to follow

the slaves he no longer controlled but not by change, hell, no, just away from this dark and frozen city.

He walked to the limits of his domain and was flung violently and painfully backwards.

Quade bit back a whimper. His own defensive screen, his own canopy and he couldn't pass through it. How had the defectors—? The answer was obvious, they still had their powers and perhaps outside help.

He knew that his armoury of formidable weapons were useless to penetrate it. He had made sure of that himself.

*'Neither we nor any power in the universe can help you.'*

Quade sat down on the frozen ground and tried to figure it out. He knew he had part of the answer. One could not go on taking out forever. It was like over-cultivation and now he was paying for it. He had created a dust bowl which choked everything and produced nothing.

He was well aware that commands were brought about by a mechanism in his mind and he saw what he had done —overworked it. Muscles failed when they were strained and even machines broke down through over-use.

In sudden brief clarity he perceived an inner law. The mechanism was strengthened by positive use and weakened by the wholly negative. He had used his negatively but those bastard do-gooders had used theirs to enrich others.

Quade rose from the damp ground in a fury of frustration. 'Blast them! *Blast* them!'

He wished the fury and hatred behind the words had force but he knew they hadn't. They wouldn't even *know* he had wished them dead.

He began to walk slowly back to the city, noting the icy wind and the decaying buildings. He knew as he walked that it would have made no difference had he escaped. He understood now, although obscurely, that somehow the icy cold and the prevailing decay was his inner self reflected outwardly. Wherever he went, these sort of conditions would go with him because he couldn't escape from himself.

He clenched and unclenched his hands desperately in his pockets. There was nothing he could do, he could not even wish himself dead. He knew he could never generate enough courage to put a gun to his head or a knife to his throat. He was stuck here—forever. At the height of his powers, he had been fool enough to bestow upon himself *immortality*—

Quade was not the only one in trouble. Far out in space, the Asdrake fleet was still heading in blissful ignorance towards Earth.

Such an attitude of mind was about to be rudely interrupted. The Supreme Commander after a long comfortable sleep was about to sit down at his desk for a brief spell of duty.

The duty did not amount to much, a few memos from various sections of the fleet to attend to and little more.

The memos were always forwarded in small brown envelopes of which 'communications' had an abundance.

As he lowered himself into the chair, however, something caught his attention. One of the envelopes was a bright and, to him, a repellent shade of red.

He twitched his tail angrily out of the way of his descending body and scowled at the envelope. If some rating were developing into a comedian, he must be executed. Lack of respect to a superior was a capital offence.

He picked up the envelope and ripped it open. The printed message inside was brief and offensive.

*'You see yourselves as warrior race embarked on the conquest of singularly obscure galaxy. To place the picture in its proper perspective you are a race of spatial maggots devouring each world as you come to it. You have never fought a full scale battle against a worthwhile adversary in your entire history. More to the point, however, your petty conquests have disrupted the order of a superior intelligence and for this you must now pay.'*

The Supreme Commander's body sagged over the desk. The printed message despite altogether crude contempt had an inner message inside it.

There was no need to ask if it came from some space-mad rating in communications, he *knew* it hadn't. It had come from far beyond the galaxy and its purpose was punitive. Somehow he, the Supreme Commander had blundered into the affairs of a highly advanced race. He had blundered, the fleet had blundered through no fault of their own but still had to pay.

He straightened in his chair, short of breath, his long tongue lolling as if from excessive heat.

He had better inform the Second in Command, no perhaps not.

The Second in Command already had the message. He must inform the Supreme Commander immediately—wait, careful now. Perhaps he was the only member of the fleet to receive it. In which case, he could well be disciplined, even executed for creating alarm and despondency. He couldn't *prove* that the message came from beyond the galaxy, could he?

Down below decks, a lowly rating was desperately trying to decide which side of the store room to clean first. He couldn't make up his mind—

It took the Supreme Commander nearly an hour to decide what the message had done—*it had taken away his power of decision.* From hereon no orders would be carried out because he lacked the power to give them. Within the fleet, no one did anything, no one could come to a decision—.

## CHAPTER ELEVEN

Travers and Lisa were walking by the lake, periodically they threw a branch into the water and Obar plunged in to retrieve it.

They were, however, talking seriously.

'Perhaps I'm a little dumb,' said Lisa. 'But I fail to see how a highly advanced technology can equal us.'

He nodded. 'I've given some thought to that subject myself. I can see some of it. I suppose with micro-engineering a lot of button-size units could be cooked up. A unit to control the weather locally, a matter-transmitter to transport instantly or an anti-gravity device for personal levitation. I suppose, given advanced electronics one could tune-in to the electrical output of the brain and have yourself a form of telepathy.'

He frowned thoughtfully. 'That gives me an—'

She laid her hand quickly on his arm before he could finish the sentence.

'Look at Obar.'

He saw that the dog had frozen itself on the edge of the water, nose thrust forward, one leg slightly raised.

'He's pointing. He sees or senses something we can't. You know, it never occurred to me that he might be one up on us as regards certain faculties.'

'Look!' she said, quickly.

About ten feet in front of the dog, there was a curious distortion in the atmosphere and then something began to form.

Obar's fur rose briefly along his back and then lowered. He relaxed slowly and wagged his tail.

'It's friendly anyway,' he said.

'It doesn't look friendly,' she said doubtfully. 'To me it looks like an outsize jelly fish.'

As they approached, the 'jelly fish' drew itself up into a kind of cone-shape and from something vaguely repellent, became oddly beautiful. It swirled with smoky colour but of such range, subtlety, and delicate variation that they were both moved emotionally.

Travers cautiously opened his mind just enough for normal conversation.

'Who are you?'

'We do not bestow names but, for your convenience, will invent something—how about Astril?'

'Fine, may I ask what you want?'

'I am not sure that I want anything. Curiosity brings me to this world. I was anxious to meet the entity who broadcasts baseless accusations—I am one of your ten suspects.'

'If you're innocent, what's the problem?'

'The problem is that you're causing my race considerable discomfort indirectly.'

'I apologize for that but it was unavoidable.'

'I appreciate your problem but it does nothing to help my race. With all due modesty, I believe, we were a respected and not unpopular people. Now we are suspect intelligence which we find hurtful.'

'As I said before, if you are innocent—'

'We are innocent but I have no intention of opening my mind to prove it.'

'No,' said Travers, firmly. 'I, myself, would regard that as an impertinence. I will open mine or, more aptly, ours.'

It seemed, for a few seconds, a cool wind blew inside his head which slowly changed to a warmth and deep understanding. Astril's colours were now even more exquisite.

'Apologies, I now see *your position.* The threat which hangs over your race and the suffering already endured justifies your act.'

There was a slight pause and inferences of embarrassment.

'I hope you'll forgive me but I nicked a few things from your minds. I'll erase them from my memory if you object.'

'Pardon?' Travers was amused and puzzled.

'Well, my idiom, "nicked" in preference to the honest "stolen" is one example. There was also to illustrate—

*Before the beginning of years,*
*There came to the making of man—*

Shall I continue? I learned from your minds that I am quoting from Swinburne. This is beautiful verse you know. I also took lines from Edgar Allen Poe and quite a few more.'

Travers understood suddenly. Here was a creative race, no doubt poets, artists, musicians and art had always been international, now apparently it was universal. Any race, however lowly, could produce work which could be appreciated by the highest.

'Take all you wish,' he said. 'I am no musician but there are melodies in my memory also.'

'I play the piano moderately well,' said Lisa. 'Oh and yes, we'll put you in touch with Pabst. He's a cultured man, knows the major German poets backwards.'

They felt a rush of warm appreciation, then, 'My friends, I will open my mind to you.'

They saw, within seconds, that Astril's race was blameless. Acts of violence were abhorrent to them.

As Astril departed well pleased about an hour later, they received a call from Akron.

'It is only fair to tell you that the Asdrake fleet has paid the penalty for its blunder as I foresaw. It is now drifting helplessly because every living being throughout has lost the power of decision.'

Travers did not hesitate. 'I cannot permit that. We are not a vindictive people and I take exception to our enemies doing the job for us.'

He paused. 'You have told me the rules, Akron, I shall not break them but I'm not going to treat these creeps as if they were little boys. They're not going to be patted on the head and told not to do it again.'

'What are you going to do?'

'They understand a show of force. They're going to get one, I'm going to put the frighteners on them.'

'Very well.'

Travers caught the undertones of faint amusement and grinned at Lisa. 'Let's have a little conference before we start, my darling—.'

The Supreme Commander's pink tongue hung almost to his desk, he was panting noisily and unable to see the opposite wall of his stateroom.

The lights were dim and the air was foul. He knew he should give orders to correct the situation but he was unable to do so. Suppose he gave the orders and overloaded the emergency generators. Suppose some incompetent rating pressed the wrong button. If only he could—

Something seemed to hit him suddenly inside his head and he jerked erect. He *knew* what to do, he had always known what to do but he had been unable to reach a decision.

He began to bark orders into the intercom. The lights brightened almost immediately and fresh air began to replace the stale.

Below decks, a lowly rating began to sweep busily. He now knew which place to begin.

The Supreme Commander finished issuing orders and

looked up. His fur rose stiffly and his thick lips drew back exposing his fangs.

Facing him, upright but apparently relaxed was a puny-looking hairless biped.

The Race of Asdrake was not parapsychic and never would be. The Supreme Commander had no means of knowing that the creature he saw was wholly subjective. It appeared that he saw it, so he concluded it was there.

Again, when it spoke later, he had no means of knowing that the communication was telepathic. As far as he was concerned, it spoke to him fluently in his own tongue.

The Supreme Commander had always flattered himself that he knew what to do in an emergency. He drew his ugly ceremonial side-arm and pointed it threateningly.

'Explain your presence here.'

'Social,' said the biped pleasantly. 'I think it's about time we had a little chat.'

The other's eyes narrowed and the furry feline ears flattened angrily.

'Who do you think you are? I could kill you where you stand.'

'If you feel like that, by all means have a go but then you will never know who I am, will you?'

The other controlled his temper with considerable effort. 'Very well, who are you?'

The biped showed him its small white teeth. 'I am one of the victims of your bio-chemical missiles. Or, to explain it another way, I am from the world you are on your way to occupy. If you care to call your alio-anthropologist, he will confirm it. By the way, you were warned, weren't you? Your department of Bio-chemical Warfare did suggest you abort for further research but you knew best as usual. You're sadly lacking in imagination, Supreme Commander.'

The other, feeling his temperature rising, pulled the trigger. No one, *no one*, needled *him*.

He watched the six blue bolts of energy pass harmlessly through the puny biped and splash noisily on the resistant bulkhead behind.

A cold feeling clutched at his insides, bringing with it an uncharacteristic caution. Perhaps he'd better play this creature along until he knew what its game was.

'You finished?' enquired the biped politely, 'or have you something else you'd like to try out?'

When the other didn't answer he said: 'Good, you will assemble your chief officers, the alio-anthropologist and all other pertinent experts in the ship's conference room within ten minutes. I will then tell you why I am here.'

The Supreme Commander, slowly regaining his confidence said: 'Why should I?' And, angrily, 'Are you daring to give *me* orders?'

'I am and you will obey them.'

The ceremonial weapon in the other's hand suddenly puffed smoke and burned fragments fell to the desk.

'The next time you point a weapon at me, your hand will go with it, understand? Yes, I am giving you orders and these orders you will obey. Ten minutes from now, clear?'

There was consternation in the conference room. The staff had not been told why they had been directed there and the Supreme Commander was morose and silent. They assumed it was an enquiry into the recent failure of the life-support systems and the peculiar indecision which had afflicted them for a long period.

When Travers appeared, fur stiffened and ears flattened angrily.

'Tell those present the type of lifeform I am and from which world I come.' The words were addressed to the alio-anthropologist.

The expert was shocked. He was an aging creature with many bald patches but retained for his outstanding ability.

'This is a Human,' he said in a quavering frightened voice. 'It comes from the world we have attacked.'

'Thank you. I think that is proof enough. I will now tell you what those missiles did and why certain lifeforms took exception to your dreams of conquest.'

He gave them a brief outline and made a swift survey of their minds.

'I see the majority of you accept the outline but repudiate, contemptuously the parapsychic angle. Very well, you shall have proof, how about this?'

He made a deliberately theatrical gesture with his right hand and suddenly there was a long bronze-coloured cylinder on the conference table.

Fur rose, lips were drawn back and they surged backwards. Several tried the exit doors and found them jammed.

'You know what this is?' Travers addressed the Supreme Commander.

The other stopped his tongue lolling by an effort of will.

'It's a solar bomb.'

'One of yours, I think. Anyone got nerve enough to come and read the number?'

After a long pause, a junior officer came forward shakily. 'One, two, stroke, six, five, four,' he read out.

'Correct. Ask your fleet commanders to check their bomb bays.'

The officer did so and finally an alarmed voice said that one solar device was missing.

'Ask him to check the number,' said Travers.

The officer complied and a shaky voice through the speaker said: 'One, two, stroke, six, five, four.'

Travers smiled at them unpleasantly. 'I can't imagine why you are all pressing yourselves against the wall. You should know the power of this thing far better than I. However, I'd say if this thing blows, it will not only take this ship but your entire fleet. Let's see now, this small screw activates the device, I believe.'

The screw began to turn slowly, apparently of its own volition.

Eyes bulged, tails rose stiffly and then someone cracked.

'Please, Honoured One, *please.* I bow to your mastery but please, no further. The arming device is highly sensitive and inclined to instability.'

The screw stopped turning and the protester went limp.

'You dislike it here?' Travers smiled. 'Perhaps you would prefer it here.'

A blank wall was slowly transformed into a picture of Keklis, capital city of their home world.

'No!' The Supreme Commander was on his feet. 'The city is defenceless. It is filled with our females and our young.'

Travers nodded. 'Point two three of your entire population. Indirectly your missiles accounted for three-quarters of Earth's people and not even in honest combat.'

The Supreme Commander cringed not only physically but mentally. It was now impossible to refute the truth and some words from an earlier message danced accusingly in his mind. They were space maggots and had never fought a worthwhile adversary in their entire history.

He was not aware as he stood there, shorn of his arrogance, that deep within him were the seeds of better things. A spark which, perhaps, centuries hence would guide his race towards maturity.

'Detonate here,' he said stiffly, 'but spare the city.'

Travers nodded curtly. The screw rotated back to its original position and the cylinder vanished. There was an audible but cautious sigh of relief.

'Let that be a warning,' said Travers, coldly. 'And in case some of you still have doubts—.'

The long conference table split from end to end and from side to side and crashed in ruin before them.

'I could have rent this vessel in the same way, your entire fleet. Now go back and never show yourselves in this sector of space again.'

The Supreme Commander made a resigned gesture. 'As you wish but for us, all of us, either way it is death. The Ministry of War is merciless, we shall be executed for failure.'

Travers laughed softly. 'Not when I've finished with them. By the time you return, your armchair warriors will be out of office.'

He paused and looked at the other thoughtfully. 'You

are not without courage, Supreme Commander and your race is not without ingenuity. I leave with an idea. Some hours ago I was talking to one of the highest intelligences in the universe. An artistic race which abhors violence but this race, also, once had to face a population explosion. They now possess an Empire which embraces not a handful of worlds but six galaxies. They achieved this without a single conquest or the use of a single weapon, real or implied. They sent their experts to the dead worlds which abound in every galaxy. To ice-bound airless rocks, to worlds swathed in methane, any world with a suitable gravity or far enough away from its parent sun to be liveable. They turned these dead worlds into living worlds and settled there. That sort of conquest takes guts, Supreme Commander, guts, endurance, dedication and courage. It demands far more of a race than your petty little conquests which are brought about by the destruction of innocent people. Has the Race of Asdrake guts enough for this sort of conquest?'

Before the Supreme Commander's eyes, the outline of the human became transparent and then vanished completely.

In the following four days, five more of the ten accused came in to prove themselves.

'Your rather direct and undoubtedly crude approach apparently brings results,' said Akron, not without respect.

Travers nodded. 'Four left. We have enough given one item of information and four artifacts.'

'I'm afraid I don't quite understand.'

'We had a long conference about this last night. We

believe we're on to something, something decisive which we prefer to keep to ourselves at the moment.'

'What is it you require?'

'Something from one of each of the four remaining suspects. An article of clothing, say, something worn or used constantly.'

'Easily arranged. We maintain embassies on all four.'

'Lastly, one single item of information. All of these intelligences must reproduce in one form or another whether it be artificially or naturally. We wish to know which of these four is exceedingly touchy about the process, perhaps maintaining guards of some kind to keep out the curious and unauthorized.'

The alien nodded. 'I will look into the matter immediately.'

'Discreetly, please. You have been a good friend to us and we don't want you involved.'

'I am already involved, my friends, my assistance was no doubt noted by your enemies as soon as it began. I was responsible for discovering that someone had broken the rules.'

'All this we know, old friend, but this is our fight now. We don't want you hurt in it.'

'I propose staying to see it through, regardless.'

Travers laughed. 'I am tempted to clap you heartily on your assumed back. I must warn you, however, that you may be shocked. The condition in which the enemy placed us, taught us one thing, it taught us to fight. Our methods may strike you as provocative and crude in the extreme.'

An hour later, the four articles arrived. The first was an obvious piece of clothing which was never intended to fit anything remotely human. The second was a circle of metal which seemed to have no obvious purpose. Unless, thought Travers, this particular race adorned itself with bangles. He didn't try with the third. It was a green, T-shaped object, the purpose of which defied the imagination.

The fourth looked like the middle of a belt and was covered in small yellow stones.

Travers looked at his friends and reached for Lisa's hand. 'First I want to try something.'

He whistled mentally and Obadiah came bounding in at the door a few seconds later.

'Sit!' He laid the articles carefully out on the floor. 'Listen Obar, one of these things over here hates us, follow?'

He knew that Obar understood for although the sentence sounded odd, it was direct to the animal's reasoning.

'I want you to see if you can tell which one.'

The dog rose, crossed the room and began to sniff the articles cautiously. At the fourth, the fur rose on his back and he growled deep in his throat.

Travers patted him affectionately. 'You're a good old door mat, aren't you?'

He picked up the thing which looked like part of a belt and held it for a second or so. Then he handed it to Robinson. 'Don't tell me your findings, pass it on, this is an independent check to see if we all arrive at the same answer. The last to receive gives the first answer.'

Nasuki was the last and he held the belt only briefly.

'This thing belongs to a race calling itself the Kroyne.' He dropped the belt on the floor and kicked it away with his foot. 'They are semi-humanoid in appearance. Short legs, squat sort of bodies and big bulging heads. They look kind of top-heavy.'

Travers looked at the others. 'Well?'

'Correct in all detail. We got the same picture.'

He smiled. 'If my guess is correct, their top-heavy appearance is indicative.'

Akron entered at that moment. 'I have the information you require.'

'May we anticipate you? The race which keeps its infants under a close guard is the Kroyne.'

Akron was shaken out of his usual calm. 'How did you know that?'

Travers told him. 'This is the guilty race. What can you tell us about them?'

Akron was briefly silent as if considering his answer. 'On reflection, not a great deal. They are the oldest and most powerful of all. They controlled an Empire before most of the known intelligences in the universe had formed a stable culture. The Mulda, an aquatic race are the second oldest but the Kroyne had an empire before the Mulda became amphibious. As far as is known, their conduct has always been beyond reproach. They are a parapsychic race but shield themselves very little.'

'As far as is known,' said Travers thoughtfully. 'Only they had about thirty billion years to run amok before there was anyone around to note the fact. I'll add a rider to that too, if there was, they've been removed.'

'What you say is possible.'

'Correction, friend, more than probable.'

'Perhaps. What is your next move?'

'Something you won't care for, we're going to provoke them into ill-considered action or a false move.'

'How will you do that?'

'A little device called rumour. We have many friends and sympathizers in the universe now. We are going to tell these friends that we believe the Kroyne to be the guilty race.'

'Suppose you are mistaken?'

'We don't think we are but if so, our suspects will rapidly be reduced to three.'

Akron appeared to meditate briefly, then he said, 'I am inclined to share your opinion but I am unhappy, distinctly unhappy on your behalf. Have you, please, the remotest conception of what you are pitting yourself against? If your conclusions are correct you are baiting an enemy so highly skilled in duplicity that he fooled the highest intelligences in the universe for millions of years. A ruthless enemy who, in terms of power, could crush your little planet to dust between finger and thumb. His empire covers forty-eight galaxies and his numbers exceed the imagination.'

'We are aware of the dangers,' said Travers soberly, 'but we think he has an Achilles heel.'

Rumour has an insidious habit of not only spreading rapidly but penetrating the most unlikely places. Within a short time every intelligence in the universe had heard it. It was passed on, not because such intelligences were prone to gossip but because, by their very natures, they liked to reason, discuss and draw logical conclusions.

'The Humans have directly accused the Kroyne.'

'They will refute the accusation, of course.'

'No doubt, but they have not yet done so.'

The committee was advised and a special emissary appointed who met Travers personally.

'I assure you, your charges are groundless. I have visited the Kroyne personally. They opened their minds to me completely. They have nothing to conceal.'

'In which case,' said Travers reasonably. 'Why can't they open their minds to us? If I am mistaken, I will apologize before the entire universe and you may place that on record.'

The emissary went away with a nagging doubt. Why not indeed? Five races had already done so and had not only gained respect by so doing but had reported favourably on the humans.

He decided unhappily that unless the Kroyne complied soon, there was only one answer. The humans possessed a faculty lacking in other parapsychic races. The Kroyne knew about it and couldn't afford to take the risk. They had discovered the possibility millions of cycles ago and tried to muffle it without being detected in the process.

He reported the possibility reluctantly to the committee but other races had already drawn the same conclusions.

Pressure built up against the Kroyne and there was a marked coolness in diplomatic relations and other contacts. In many cases distrust was pointed.

The Kroyne had never been well liked, they were aloof by nature, but they had been respected if only for their venerability.

The top beings who controlled the mighty Kroyne empire realized that time was running out fast. If they didn't do something, guilt would be automatically assumed and if they did—they had to think of something and fast.

# CHAPTER TWELVE

'I think,' said Pabst, 'our command had better embrace the whole planet.'

Travers nodded quickly. 'I'd thought of that also. Every blade of grass, natural or alien, every living thing. I hope to God I'm right—about their Achilles heel, I mean. If I'm not, we've had it.'

He stared across the small lake. The scene looked very different from nearly a year ago. It was now early Summer and on the opposite side of the lake had been a flat, grassy sort of meadow. The terrain was the same, the meadow stretched for about a mile before rising slowly to the distant hills. It was the meadow which had changed, much of the grass was a soft and pastel blue. Bushes and plants had grown, tall and slender trees had climbed skywards, some at the incredible rate of eighteen inches a day. Neither plants, bushes or trees had begun their life on Earth but somehow they had contrived to fit into the ecology. Normal birds nested in them and a variety of insects seemed to find them as nourishing as normal trees. A large number were incredibly beautiful with a delicacy of colour which would have been a challenge to any artist.

Travers saw them and somehow didn't see them. Out there in that more or less open ground, the Kroyne deputation had elected to present themselves within an hour.

'Why sixty?' enquired Robinson worriedly. 'It's the hell of a lot isn't it?'

'The reason given,' said Pabst heavily, ' is a cross-section of their culture. We may look into their minds and know that *all* are guiltless. I agree with Dave's unspoken anxiety, however, it's sixty to four or sixty to eight according to viewpoint.'

'Sixty to four,' said Lisa firmly.

'Are we over-dramatizing the situation?' enquired Nasuki. 'I have no doubt there will be observers, what can they *do*?'

'Only one thing,' said Robinson quietly. 'Demonstrate their powers of duplicity. It's reasonable to assume they'll try and discredit us.'

'And having done so,' said Pabst. 'They can afford to sit back and take their time, the long-term elimination of an upstart and inferior culture. When do you think they'll strike?'

Travers laughed harshly. 'That's an easy one, before we get a chance to look into their minds.'

He kissed Lisa's cheek gently. 'Guess we'd better start walking, by the time we get to the meeting place they should be due.'

The eight/four walked unhurriedly by the lake side, furtively bringing up the rear and against orders came Obadiah.

The animal felt slightly guilty but it justified its actions on the grounds of necessity. It sensed danger and if there was danger it had to be there. It would be necessary to remain hidden but close enough to go into action.

Travers was aware of flutterings of fear inside him and knew it applied to the others.

Somehow the stress had heightened his awareness of the beauty around him. The sun sparkling on the waters of the lake, the tiny alien flowers in the grass and the yellow of normal buttercups:

*—where the buttercup*
*Had blessed with gold their slow boots coming up,*
*Where even little brambles would not yield*
*But clutched and clung to them like sorrowing hands.*

He wondered if Astril had those lines and knew that the words were far truer now than when they had been written.

Many of the slender alien trees leaned towards them caressingly as they passed. Birds circled them as they walked. Mankind was rapidly establishing an empathy with his entire planet, normal as well as alien.

As they reached the end of the lake, there was a flickering at far limits of the meadow. Figures appeared, too far away as yet to see in detail.

The figures formed into lines and began to march towards them.

'Five spaced lines of twelve apiece,' observed Robinson. 'Very neat and precise.'

'I would describe it another way,' said Pabst. 'I would call it battle order.'

'In front of observers we cannot see but know they are here?'

'Why not? We are dealing with the most advanced exponents of treachery in the universe.'

When a bare hundred feet separated the two parties, a needle of white fire appeared to leap from Robinson's forehead and four of the Kroyne crumpled to the ground.

It was a signal for the rest to break for cover and as they did so, observers appeared. Some looked humanoid and some didn't try to.

The Kroyne took refuge behind them.

'The humans attacked us, you all saw. It was their intention all along, we *knew*. They are barbarians and disrupters.'

Travers came forward, tense but unhurriedly.

'Of what are you accusing us?'

'You have killed four of our kind.'

Travers smiled grimly. 'Will some observer please check the dead.'

A thing which looked like a swirling mist moved to the prone bodies.

'There are no dead here,' it reported. 'They are traumatically shocked but in no way injured.'

'Naturally they are shocked,' said Travers. 'Their own kind were prepared to sacrifice them ruthlessly in order to place the blame on us.'

He looked at the nearest Kroyne. 'It hasn't worked, creep, a shielded micro-weapon is a brilliant idea, particularly so when it appears to come from us. Fortunately we figured you'd do something like this. I raised a barrier, not to protect us but you. The observers will confirm.'

'We came with good intent. We saw that competent observers looked into our minds before departure. Their testimony you cannot refute.'

'Care to bet?' enquired Pabst from behind Travers.

The Kroyne's high forehead crinkled into a scowl. 'Your aim was treachery.'

'So you say, proving it is another thing. Let any one of the present observers—not us—look into your minds now.'

'As you wish.'

A humanoid thing covered in a soft silvery fur came forward.

'I will do it.'

After a brief period, it said: 'I can see nothing.'

Travers said: 'No doubt, I've stopped its brain.'

The silver thing was quick. 'That is fantastic, death would follow immediately.'

'Not for a creature with two brains, one normal and one artificially constructed. Go deeper before he shuts you out.'

The silver creature drew back with detectable revulsion. 'I have seen enough.'

It was a signal for action. The Kroyne realized that their elaborate deceit had failed. The game was up, millions of years of deception had been wiped away in an instant.

A bolt of energy rushed at Travers' head but was deflected upwards. A swirling mass of fire rushed at Pabst but cannoned off and collapsed into nothingness.

A curious swirling pillar of blackness started to build up above them but never got anywhere and drifted away like smoke.

Then something happened which Travers had never anticipated—nature took a hand.

The Kroyne thought they had foreseen everything. They had prepared against the possibility of parapsychic attack and, despite its non-existence, the most advanced technology, but not the elemental.

One of the beautiful slender trees wrapped her branches about herself like a cloak and suddenly grew barbs. The barbs, eight inches in length, were suddenly ejected.

A Kroyne, fumbling with some sort of thumb-size device pitched sideways with a barb buried deep in his throat.

Another tree suddenly lashed like a whip, depositing a crumpled body twenty feet distant.

Another Kroyne, racing away in panic, ran full-tilt into a green furry thing which had been lying concealed on the ground and now rose in front of him.

He had no time to take in details, there was a low throaty growl and then the jaws closed.

Travers saw the incident out of the corner of his eye.

'Obar, you blood-thirsty old devil,' he admonished without real force.

He turned his attention to the scene in front of him. Eighteen Kroyne lay unmoving and the rest were bunched together giving an hysterical trapped feeling. Clearly they were making desperate efforts to get out from under and failing completely.

The eight/four walked towards them and they backed

away. Then apparently one of them remembered Earth history and raised his hands high above his head.

The party stopped ten feet away. 'Don't try anything,' said Travers softly. 'None of your devices will work here. You might have killed us had you been truly parapsychic but you're not, are you?'

There was a sullen silence and Travers was aware of the alien observers gathering behind them.

'About those missiles,' said Pabst conversationally. 'You know the ones I mean. You have them poised a couple of light years out in case anything went wrong. Nasty jobs, anti-matter, each one capable of deleting a galaxy. I regret to inform you that we've been compelled to move them. They are now on their way back to where they came from. Of course, six of those things won't entirely remove your empire but they won't leave a great deal.'

One of the Kroyne stepped forward. 'The mature races will never permit such destruction for any reason whatever.'

Pabst smiled broadly. 'True, very true, but then we are not going to detonate them—*you are.*'

The Kroyne looked up at him blankly.

'We detected those jobs before they arrived,' continued the German, pleasantly. 'Between us, we put in quite a lot of work but from now on they'll be cruising around your empire. They won't blow unless *you* make them. You see they're keyed to respond to aggression, treachery and your kind of complicated duplicity. I wonder how long it will be before you blow yourselves to the other end of the universe.'

'That is diabolical.'

'Yes, it is isn't it? I seem to recall that an allegedly mature race put us in a position where we had no choice but to learn that kind of thing. A good instructor, would you say?'

The fury and naked hatred of the Kroyne became almost palpable.

'We should have disposed of you from the first.'

'But you couldn't could you? You couldn't betray yourselves to races surrounding you. The cloak of respectability protected you from races you feared.'

Pabst paused and then continued. 'There is an alternative and I advise you to consider it carefully. You could start from scratch. Many, many races would be only too glad to help and in a few hundred years you could achieve true maturity.'

He turned away indifferently. 'You may leave now, if you wish. Your matter-transmitters will work now.'

Later, at the inn, there was a considerable gathering of people and alien observers.

'Once,' said Akron wistfully, 'I guided you, now it seems I must learn.'

'Wrong,' said Lisa gently and affectionately. 'You know as well as I that knowledge is not wisdom.'

'True but here you had greater knowledge.'

'Again, no,' said Travers. 'Our real asset was a more highly developed faculty. It was nothing to boast about because other parapsychic races have other faculties which are more highly developed than our own. It is like a talent, one man can compose music and another is an artist. It's just a matter of degree. We had a peculiar faculty for seeing through the Kroyne deceit, a faculty lacking in other races. They discovered that billions of years ago and did their best to shut us up forever. They knew that if we were ever permitted to develop, we could blow their cover clean away.'

'As yet we do not fully understand the deceit,' said one of the observers. 'If you would be good enough to explain.'

'I'm afraid a lot of this is guess-work,' said Travers, apologetically, 'but I think it goes something like this. In this part of the known universe, they were the first. They had achieved a high degree of technology, including space travel, long before anyone else appeared on the scene. After a few millions of years they became aware that other intelligences were occurring all around them.

'The universe was too vast and the numbers of developing intelligences too numerous for them to do anything about it. The factor which caused them most alarm however was the discovery that about a quarter of these races were parapsychic. No doubt, in these early days, a large number of these intelligences were spirited away to Kroyne worlds for study.'

Travers paused and patted Obar's head absently. 'I don't know in what order they made their discoveries but they learned to copy almost everything a parapsychic could do by technological methods.

'There were still glaring deficiencies. They were not telepathic but they had to appear telepathic. They had to be able to open their minds and close them ready for the first parapsychic race they ran up against.

'The method they arrived at was ingenious although we must not forget they had several million years in which to experiment. They built a separate brain in a laboratory with a mechanism which closely resembled the mechanism in our minds.

'I must make it quite clear that this brain, when activated, was telepathic but separated from the real brain of the Kroyne. A spurious memory and background were fed into this brain for the benefit of those who wanted to take a look.

'Satisfied, the Kroyne went into production. Every new infant was treated surgically and equipped with a double brain. One of which was laboratory constructed and contained a manipulated parapsychic mechanism.'

Travers turned to one of the observers. 'When you looked into the Kroyne mind, you looked into the artificial one as you were intended to. There you noted the pre-impressed memories, the pre-impressed goodwill, the pre-impressed innocence.'

'Of course, the additional brain didn't make the Kroyne any prettier, they had damn great heads but I suppose they thought the effort worth it. They had become one of the boys, a parapsychic race among others. They had also made themselves safe for they were fully alive to the fact that, in the event of trouble, one real adept could tear their empire to pieces.'

He smiled faintly. 'Then along came trouble. Necessity had forced them to keep a check of all developing cultures and here was one which, if allowed to develop, would betray them. They had to shut it up as quickly and as stealthily as possible. The rest you can put together for yourselves.'

'Save for one thing,' said Akron. 'How did you become aware of it?'

'Frankly, common sense or, to be impressive, a simple process of deduction. Lisa asked me how a technological culture could equal our own and that got me thinking. Then, when Grayle awakened my racial memories and I saw how they blindfolded us, one question stuck in my mind—*why a machine*? Why an oblong box when a parapsychic command could have done the job twice as effectively. When the field of suspects began to narrow, I already suspected we were dealing with a technical culture which was posing to be something else.

'It was obvious that this trick would have to begin at infancy, a process which would have to be carefully guarded. An outworlder blundering in during advanced surgery when the infant Kroyne was being fitted with his artificial telepathic brain would have blown the deceit wide open.'

One of the observers rose and bowed respectfully. 'We shall welcome you among us but what now?'

'We have a balanced society to build. In a few years we hope to be in a position to take over the education of our own children. Our new society is not quite so small as we previously feared. We have a nucleus of around sixteen million but four times that number are coming in from set-ups like Quade's where they had been enslaved.'

He paused and looked at Akron. 'I can only show those who have given so much to help us how we *feel* about it all.'

Akron bowed and changed the subject. 'A short rest is indicated.'

Travers laughed. 'Nice idea. I'll use it on a minor ambition. Lisa and I are going to try out a Rolls Royce.'

'We ought to have a celebration,' said Nasuki. 'A party perhaps.'

'With one veto,' said Robinson. 'No damn silly party games or, bet your life, some idiot will suggest one with a blindfold—.'